The Mimic

A DI Erica Swift Thriller, Volume 6

M K Farrar

Published by Warwick House Press, 2021.

This is a work of fiction. Similarities to real people, places, or events are entirely coincidental.

THE MIMIC

First edition. April 13, 2021.

Copyright © 2021 M K Farrar.

Written by M K Farrar.

Chapter One

The sharp blade slashed across his face.

Brandon Skehan gasped in alarm but managed to jerk back right at the crucial moment. Instead of the metal puncturing his eyeball, it slit his eyelid and continued to slice his temple. With horror, he struck out with his arm, and the clang of metal hitting the floor filled the darkness.

White-hot pain overwhelmed his senses, but he knew one thing. He had to run. No matter what else was happening, it was vital that he did. Blood poured down his face, blocking his vision and everything around him. He wiped the blood from his face, but it returned instantly. Blinding him. He wasn't blind though—at least he didn't think he was. The knife had missed his eye. Still the fear niggled at him—what if it hadn't? What if it had nicked him and now he'd lose his sight? No, he couldn't think about that. He had to focus on getting help.

He kept going, staggering forwards. Which way was out? If he was stumbling in the wrong direction, he'd end up at the back of the house and trapped in the walled garden instead of running out onto the street.

"Help" he cried. "Someone help me."

Brandon pushed through one door, and his heart lurched with relief. He recognised the change in smell of the shared space of the entrance hall, and the harder, colder tiled floor under foot, instead of his threadbare, moth-eaten carpet. He'd gone the right way, at least. Now all he needed to do was navigate the small space to the front door and he would make it outside.

"Help!" he shouted again.

He had an upstairs neighbour. Her name was Julie, but they'd never really had a proper conversation, only said 'hi' on passing. Perhaps she would hear his shouts and call the police. That was the best he could hope for.

His hands met with solid wood, and he patted around, unseeing, searching for a handle. Where was it? It must be here somewhere. Adrenaline surged through his veins, the pain heightening his panic. No, he couldn't let it distract him. He needed to focus. He was stronger than this.

It was a fight to stay in control.

He touched metal and yanked at the handle. To his amazement, it swung open and fresh air hit his face.

"Help!" He staggered into the street. He tried to picture where he was—he'd been living on this road for the past six months—but couldn't bring it to mind. All he could think of was the burning pain across his face and terror from the amount of blood he must have been losing. It was late—almost midnight now. What if no one was around to hear him?

A distant female voice met his ears. "Oh my God. Are you all right?"

He reached out, unseeing. "Please, there was a man. Someone cut me."

"I'll...I'll call the police." She corrected herself. "No, an ambulance." Her tone was heightened with panic, squeaky, even. But it was closer now, so she must have approached him.

He tried to open his eyes again, wanting to see what was happening, but all he saw was blood.

"Just call nine-nine-nine," he said.

"Yes, yes, of course. I'm doing it now."

Brandon pictured her, young and frightened—from the sound of her voice—holding her mobile to her ear.

"You have to be careful," he warned her. "He might come after me. He might hurt you, too."

She whimpered. "Oh God."

He didn't want to frighten her, but she needed to know. It was important.

The woman spoke. "Hello, I need an ambulance and the police. A man's been...well, cut across the face. It's really bad. He's bleeding everywhere. We need the police, too. He says another man did this to him. He might still be in the flat." A pause. "The address? Yes, we're outside of...umm...twenty-three Gainsworth Terrace in Dalston." Another pause. "Yes, please, come quickly. I can stay on the phone until you get here."

He dropped to his knees, his whole body sagging at the knowledge help was coming.

He pulled up his shirt and held the material to his ruined face. He didn't want to think about how it felt as though part of his eyelid was hanging off and there appeared to be a hole where his eyebrow used to be.

A low rumble of an engine as a car drove past, then it stopped, followed by the slam of a car door. It was too soon to be the police.

A male voice called out, "Is everything all right? What's happened?"

Followed by the young woman replying, "He's hurt, but the police and an ambulance are on their way."

A hand, warm and solid, pressed against his back. "You all right, mate? Can I do anything to help?"

Brandon didn't even want to shake his head, for the fear of opening up the wound even more. "Is the ambulance coming?"

"Yeah, it's coming," the man said. "You just hang in there."

It wasn't as though he had any choice. He clutched his shirt to his face and waited for help to arrive.

Chapter Two

B lue-and-white crime scene tape secured the front of the property. On the pavement on the other side of the cordon, a pool of blood, with a numbered crime scene marker beside it, gave way to a trail of dark spots, leading towards the front door. The two-storey house had been converted into two flats, and the attack on a man in his late twenties had happened in the ground-floor flat.

As part of the Violent Crimes Task Force, DI Erica Swift didn't only investigate murders. Knife crime was on the rise in London and had been one of the main reasons for their team being set up. She just wished they were having more of an impact on the epidemic, instead of things getting worse.

The resident of the first-floor flat hadn't been too happy about being turfed from her bed in the early hours of the morning, but until they'd had SOCO work the crime scene, including the shared entrance hall, she wouldn't be allowed back home. One of the uniformed officers was already interviewing her to find out if she'd heard or seen anything, but Erica would need to get one of her detectives to do the same. Normally, she'd have asked her sergeant, Shawn Turner, to direct the interviews, but tonight she had Acting DS Hannah Rudd with her.

Shawn had gone for a week on the Costa del Sol with a couple of mates. She'd joked with him that he could have chosen somewhere with more culture than 'Little England' in the sun, but he'd said it was exactly what he was after. She'd insisted that he at least try some Spanish food while he was out there, to which he'd cocked an eyebrow and asked if Sangria counted. When she said it didn't, he'd promised to have a couple of tapas with the booze.

Erica wished she could have gone with him. She couldn't remember the last time she'd had a real holiday. She'd taken some time off—DCI Gibbs had insisted now he was back at work—but she'd spent it locally with Poppy. They'd done a few day trips out to places, pretending to be tourists, London Zoo, Kew Gardens, a go on the London Eye. The rest of the time they'd ordered pizza and cuddled up on the sofa and watched animated films. It felt as though she got so little time to do things like this with her daughter that it had felt like a holiday, even though they hadn't stayed overnight anywhere.

A female officer walked out of the flat and approached them.

Police Sergeant Diana Reynolds was coordinating the crime scene. Erica had worked with Reynolds on several cases before.

"How are you, DI Swift?" the blonde, no-nonsense sergeant asked her.

"Good, thanks. This is Acting DS Rudd." She introduced her colleague, and the two women shook hands. "What have you got?"

"The victim is twenty-nine-year-old Brandon Skehan. He was attacked with a knife when he came home after a night out. He's been taken straight to hospital, but from the few words the responding officers managed to get from him, he didn't know who had attacked him or why. A uniformed officer went with him in the ambulance. I believe he'll need surgery."

Erica would need to speak with the victim as soon as possible, but if he was going to be taken straight into surgery, it would be some time before he came out of the anaesthesia enough to speak to her properly.

"It would appear as though whoever was responsible broke in through the back door," Reynolds continued. "It's off the kitchen and leads onto a small rear garden. We're assuming he got out that way, too, since none of the witnesses saw anyone else leaving the property."

"How many witnesses do we have?"

"Three, currently. The woman who lives upstairs, Julie Luxford, heard shouting, but she didn't come down until after the police arrived. The first person on the scene was a twenty-year-old student, Lucy Frey, who had also just got back from a night out. Good thing the incident happened just after most of the pubs kicked out. She lives across the road. She's sitting in the back of one of the squad cars, if you want to speak to her. She's pretty shaken up."

Erica nodded. "Thanks, I will. Who is the third witness?"

"Forty-two-year-old Mark Hamburg. He was also arriving home after finishing a shift at the packing plant where he works. One of my officers is sitting with him in the kitchen back at his place. Since he only arrived on the scene shortly before we did, there hasn't been much he's been able to tell us."

"Right," Erica snapped on a pair of gloves, "let's take a look at the crime scene."

They ducked beneath the tape, and Erica followed the sergeant into the flat, DS Rudd close behind. The shared entrance hall was tiny, with the door to the ground-floor flat standing open directly ahead, and the stairs leading up to the first-floor flat to their right. A radiator cover was attached to the wall and was stacked high with junk mail—leaflets offering pizza deals, advertising estate agents, or touting the local council. Droplets of blood spattered the wall above in an arc. The Scenes of Crime Officer had placed a numbered board beside it for photographing. There was another on the floor, on the threadbare carpet, beside yet more blood. She hadn't seen the victim's wound, but if it was across his face, and he'd lost this much blood, it must have been bad.

Navigating the pool of blood and the trickle that led towards—or away from—the front door, they entered the ground-floor flat. They weren't the only ones in the building; a Scenes of Crime Officer moved around, numbering anything of interest and taking photographs. He nodded at the women as they walked in.

"The victim was attacked as soon as he entered," Reynolds told them. "The attacker came from the living room, approaching the victim from behind, and reached around him to slash the knife across his face. From the little we were able to get from the victim before the ambulance took him, he hadn't even managed to turn on a light yet. He knocked the knife out of the assailant's hand and made a run for it."

The knife was still on the floor, an evidence board with a number one placed beside it. It was a five-inch blade, with a handle that looked like a regular kitchen knife.

"Did it come from the victim's kitchen?" Erica asked. "Or did the attacker bring it with them?"

"We're not sure yet."

Erica looked around, taking in every detail. "What about the rest of the flat? Was anything taken?"

Was this just a botched break-in? Or did the attacker have other motives?

"Nothing big that we can see. All the expensive technology is still here—the television and a laptop."

"The victim might have disturbed him when he got home," Acting DS Rudd suggested. "Afraid of being caught, he lashed out with the knife and made his escape."

"Yes, quite possibly." Reynolds nodded towards the back of the building. "There's a broken pane of glass in the back door where it appears as though it's been knocked in and then they reached through and opened the door from the inside."

Erica walked through the flat to the back door. Sure enough, it was just how the sergeant had described it. Glass littered the kitchen floor. She wanted to get a look outside at what would have been the attacker's escape route as well as their point of entry. The back door opened onto a narrow yard which had been illuminated with a floodlight. The paving slabs were cracked with weeds growing through them, and in need of a good power wash. A garden shed that had also seen better days, sat in the corner and a table and chairs with missing wooden slats and a rusted barbecue completed the look. A back wall led onto the garden of another house, while fences separated the yard from the adjacent neighbours.

"Has the shed been checked for anyone hiding in it?" Erica asked.

"Yes. It was one of the first things the responding officers did. No sign of anyone, though."

Erica put her hands on her hips. "Assuming the attacker both entered and escaped this way, he would have had to cross one of the neighbours' gardens. It'll be worth asking if any of them heard or saw any disturbances."

She went to the back wall, pulled herself up, and used the torch on her phone to light the garden beyond. Several dog toys and a couple of piles of shit lay on the overgrown grass. She jumped back down again.

"This household looks as though it has a dog. If he went this way, there's a good chance the dog would have started barking."

"I'll get one of my officers to go around there."

Erica walked over to the fence on the right-hand side and reached for the top and gave it a wobble. It moved at her touch, swaying back and forth. "If they'd tried to climb this side, the whole thing would have fallen down under them."

The fence on the left-hand side wasn't much better, rickety and rotting away at the base. "My guess is he went over the wall and must have gained access the same way, too." It could be an important lead. "I'll walk around and have a chat with the owner, find out if he saw or heard anything. I want to talk to the young woman first, though. You said her name was Lucy Frey?"

Reynolds nodded. "That's right."

Erica turned to her acting sergeant. "Rudd, can you speak to the upstairs neighbour?"

Rudd nodded. "Right away, boss."

Hannah Rudd had been thrilled to get the opportunity to step into Shawn's shoes while he was away. It had caused a bit of tension in the office, particularly with DC Howard, who'd thought he should have been chosen for the job, but Rudd had been sharp and enthusiastic the whole time, and Erica knew she hadn't made the wrong choice.

Erica left the property and walked over to the police car where the first witness was sitting in the back seat, the rear door open. A female uniformed officer was with her, crouched to bring them to the same level, speaking in a low, calm tone that Erica struggled to catch.

The young woman barely looked old enough to be living by herself, never mind be out in the early hours of the morning. She was twenty—apparently—but could have passed for sixteen. She held a cup of water in one hand, but it was shaking so badly she was in danger of throwing it all over herself, and her face was pale.

Erica took out her ID as she approached and showed it. "Hi, Lucy. I'm DI Swift. I wondered if I could have a quick word?"

The uniformed officer gave her a nod of acknowledgement and rose to standing. "I'll be right over there if you need me."

"Thanks," Erica said and then turned her attention to the witness. "I hear you were the first one to find Mr Skehan this evening."

Lucy nodded. "I wouldn't say I found him, exactly. Saw him, would be a better way of saying it. He burst out of the house, yelling for help and covered in blood. I was on my way home, but it wasn't like I could just ignore him or anything, so I ran over to help."

"Where were you on your way home from?"

"A pub in Stratford. A friend's band was playing, and I went to watch."

"What time did you leave the pub?"

Lucy frowned as she thought. "About eleven. I got the Tube home and walked the rest of the way."

Erica glanced back to the victim's flat. "Have you ever met Mr Skehan before?"

"No, I haven't. I've seen him occasionally from my window, coming and going, but that's all."

"You live nearby?"

Lucy pointed across the road. "Yes, just over there. Number forty-two."

Erica recounted what she'd been told. "So, you were on your way home from a pub in Stratford where you'd been watching a friend play in a band. You caught the Tube and walked the rest of the way to your house when you came across Mr Skehan. Can you describe what you saw?"

"I was on the other side of the street. He had his hands over his face, and blood was pouring out from between his fingers and running down his shirt. I didn't know what had happened. I thought he might have had an accident of some kind, but then he started shouting about there being a man in his flat and that it was dangerous, and I needed to be careful."

"Did you see anyone?"

She shook her head. "No. He'd left the front door open, so I did check because I was frightened, but I didn't see anyone. The inside of the flat was dark, though, and it was hard to see much of anything."

"What about before you saw Mr Skehan? Did you notice anything unusual? Any strange people hanging around or any different cars on the street?"

"No, nothing like that. Everything was normal."

"What about during the days before the attack? Did you notice anyone or anything unusual?"

"No, sorry. I wish I could be of more help."

Erica gave her a reassuring smile. "You have been helpful, Lucy." She handed her a business card. "Call me if you think of anything, though. Even if it seems small and insignificant, I still want to know. It could make all the difference in finding who did this."

Lucy looked down at the card. "I will." She bit her lower lip. "Can I ask you something?"

"Absolutely."

"Do you think the person who did this will come after me? I mean, if he thinks I might have seen him and would be able to identify him, he might decide that I'm next."

"That's unlikely, Lucy," Erica assured her. "First of all, the attacker never came out the front of the house, so he wouldn't have seen you. Secondly, even if the attacker did see you, he wouldn't know anything about you. He wouldn't know where you live or what your name is, or anything like that. It won't do any harm for you to be on your guard, though. If you're feeling unsafe, call us."

The girl nodded. "Okay, thank you."

"It's understandable to be shaken up. We have contacts within the Victim's Support Service one of my officers can put you in touch with who can offer you support."

She hiccupped a sob. "I think I'm going to need that."

"Not a problem. That's what we're here for."

Rudd had also finished speaking to the upstairs neighbour, and Erica turned to her as she approached. "Can you go and talk to the other witness, Mr Hamburg? I want to go and check out the house that this one backs onto."

Rudd nodded. "Of course."

Erica walked to the end of the street, took a left, then left again, to bring herself onto the road that ran behind the victim's flat. She kept going until she reached the correct property, the police lights behind the building giving her an indication as to which was the right one. The house was in darkness, so either no one was in, or she was about to wake someone up.

She rang the doorbell and moved back. From inside, loud barking started, followed by the shout of a man telling the dog to shut up. A light came on inside the house. Clearly, all the activity in the street behind them hadn't been enough to keep them awake. She felt a little guilty at waking someone in the early hours of the morning, but it couldn't wait.

The door opened, and an overweight man in a pair of boxer shorts and a white vest rubbed at his eyes. "Do you know what time it is?"

"Sorry to disturb you. My name is DI Swift, and I'm investigating an incident that occurred in the property behind yours. I'm afraid I need to ask you a couple of questions." She held out her ID.

He squinted at it. "I don't know anything about that."

"I'll need to be the judge of that, Mr...?"

"Bennett. Roy Bennett."

Behind him, a large Alsatian pushed with his head to get past its owner's bare legs. He held it back by the animal's collar. "This is Ruby. She looks scary, but she won't hurt you."

"That's okay, Mr Bennett. Dogs don't worry me. I'd like to ask you some questions and I need to take a look at your back garden."

"I suppose that's okay," he grumbled, moving out of the way to let her through. As with the victim's house, there was no side entrance to the garden.

"What's happened then?" he asked.

"A man was attacked with a knife in his home."

Roy Bennett tutted. "Jesus. Don't know what's wrong with kids these days."

"To be fair," Erica said, "we don't know how old the assailant was."

"Bound to be kids. Always is lately. They like their knives, too, don't they? Act like it's cool to try and destroy someone else's life. I blame the parents, personally. They're all too busy on their phones or getting drunk or God knows what else to give a shit about what their kids are up to."

Erica didn't think there was much point in trying to explain to him once more that there weren't necessarily any kids involved with this case. Besides, she didn't like how everyone blamed teenagers for everything these days. After all, the teenagers were being brought up by parents who had had parents themselves, so all the problems couldn't be put down to one generation, or even two.

"If you could just show me the back garden."

He led her through the small, slightly grubby house. The walls were covered in textured wallpaper that was peeling in the corners, and the floor looked as though it hadn't been hoovered in a very long time. They passed through a galley kitchen leading onto the back door. It was a similar layout to the victim's place, only this property had remained as a house and hadn't been divided into flats.

The back door key stuck out of the lock. Just like in the victim's house, the top half of the door was a pane of glass.

Erica nodded at the key. "You shouldn't leave that in the lock overnight. It makes it easy for people to break in."

He shrugged. "Who'd want to break in here? Nothing to steal. Besides, then they'd have to face Ruby."

The dog probably was more of a deterrent than anything else. Erica figured that if she was ever going to choose somewhere to break into, she'd go with the property that didn't have the huge, barking dog. Most dogs could be easily distracted with a decent bone, though, or a really determined criminal wouldn't hesitate to resort to violence to dispose of a pet.

Bennett opened the back door and stepped out.

"If I can just ask you to wait here for me, Mr Bennett," she said, moving past him. "I'm not sure yet if the man we're after is still around, and if he's left any clues for us, I need to make sure they're not disturbed." She glanced up at the outside wall, hoping to see a security camera. There wasn't one, but there was an external light.

"And can you flick the switch for the outside light as well," she asked.

The dog must have decided it was time to go out, but the owner grabbed her by the collar, preventing her from following Erica. Bennett did as she'd asked and turned on the light, a bright white glow illuminating the back garden.

"Mind the grass," he said. "There's dog shit on it."

Lovely.

Erica turned her attention to the small space, assessing it for any possibility someone might still be hiding there. There wasn't much to the garden—a patch of weed-blown grass, a flowerbed around the edges that contained a few shrubs. A handful of flowers bravely popped their heads from between the weeds.

She used the torch on her phone to check for any signs that the man had come this way, but there was nothing obvious. She needed to make sure SOCO went over the garden as thoroughly as the house.

Erica turned back to the house and dodged a large mound of dog mess, just missing it at the last minute. She was too late to stop the 'ugh' of dismay bursting from her mouth.

"Sorry," Bennett commented. "Didn't know I was going to have to clean it for people in the middle of the night."

"You don't need to clean anything up, Mr Bennett. In fact, I'm specifically asking you not to touch anything. I'm going to need to get my forensics team around here. We might be able to pick up a shoe print or even fibres off the wall. I'm going to need to ask that both you and the dog stay out of the garden until they're done."

His doughy face grew even more sullen. "What if she needs a piss?"

"You'll have to take her for a walk, Mr Bennett." She smiled sweetly. "I'm sure that won't be too much of an inconvenience for you."

He harrumphed in irritation. "She's gonna bark her head off the whole time if there's people messing around out there."

"Does she bark a lot then?"

"Yeah, whenever anyone is near the house. Drives me up the bloody wall. I shout at her to tell her to shut up, but she just thinks I'm barking as well. Probably reckons I'm joining in."

Erica frowned. "But she didn't bark this evening?"

"Well, she did when you arrived."

"What about earlier than that? Around eleven-thirty?"

He shook his head. "Don't think so, but then I would have been half asleep at that time."

That was odd. If a stranger had jumped into the back garden and the dog normally barked when people were around, why hadn't it barked this time? Unless the assailant was just very light on his feet, and the dog simply didn't hear him. It was possible, of course, or perhaps the owner was sound asleep and didn't hear the dog barking. There was no way for her to know for certain.

"And you're sure you haven't seen anyone hanging around lately? Any strange cars parked in the street?"

"No, I haven't. Everything's been normal." He paused and then added, "The bloke who was attacked, is he going to be okay?"

"I hope so, Mr Bennett."

"Good."

"My team will be with you shortly," she said. "Don't touch anything out there."

"I won't," he promised.

She left via the front door and stepped back out onto the pavement. The road was made up of terraced houses, the same as on the victim's street. The only way the attacker could have got out was through the neighbours' gardens. Hopefully, one of them would have seen or heard something that would give them a lead.

Chapter Three
Two years earlier

• • • •

THE DOOR OF THE PRISON cell swung shut, an electronic buzzing filling Nicholas Bailey's ears, signalling the door was locked.

Was this going to be his home for the rest of his adult life? A fourteen-foot by ten-foot room, containing only a set of bunk beds, an exposed toilet—there would be no privacy in this place—a solid plastic chair, a shelf and cupboard, and a wash basin. The barred window looked out on the exercise yard beyond, a view of yet more grey upon grey.

"Make yourself comfortable, Bailey," Prison Officer Ian Bache said through the little hatch. "You're going to be here for a very long time."

In the bottom bunk, a skinny white man with a hooked nose and deep-set eyes swung his legs off the side and sat up. He wore the same prison-issued outfit of a grey sweatshirt and jogging bottoms that Nicholas had on. Together with Velcro trainers, since no shoelaces were allowed at the risk of them being used as a ligature. Behind the man, posters of women in suggestive poses had been stuck to the wall with now hardened toothpaste as glue wasn't allowed.

"You're my new roommate, huh?" He scowled in Nicholas's direction. "You'd better not cause me any trouble."

Nicholas straightened his shoulders and lifted his chin, doing his best not to appear afraid. He didn't have much knowledge of prison life, but he knew that. Showing your fear was like waving a red flag.

The skinny man jerked his chin. "You gonna tell me your name or just stand there like a faggot?"

"Nicholas," he replied. "My name's Nicholas Bailey."

Recognition lit the other man's face, and a smile spread across it, exposing a set of crooked teeth. He pointed a finger. "Wait a minute. You're the one who's been all over the news, ain't you? The psycho who killed that cop's husband."

The knot inside Nicholas's chest unravelled a fraction. "Yeah, that's me."

His new bunkmate brayed laughter and slapped his thighs. "Good on you, mate. You did some other sick stuff, too, right? Cut out peoples' eyes and shit like that?"

For some reason, Nicholas squirmed inside at those details. It was personal, that was why. What had happened between him and the people he'd chosen shouldn't have been made public knowledge. But he wasn't stupid and if he needed to use what he'd done to make his life easier, then he would.

He cleared his throat and jutted out his jaw. "I might have done."

"Wait till the others hear about this. I bet you've got some good stories in you, too. Life is fucking boring in here, so we always like to get the gory details off anyone who isn't going to try hiding behind the whole 'innocent' bullshit. Ain't none of us innocent in here, if even some of us didn't commit the crimes we were accused of. Guaranteed we did something else that would have landed us behind bars."

"What did you do to end up here?" Nicholas dared to ask.

"Me? I didn't do nothin'. I'm innocent!" And he set off in that braying laugh again.

Nicholas balled his fists, his nails digging into his palms with sharp stings of pain. That laugh was already grating on him, and he potentially had years of listening to it. Unless something unfortunate happened to his cellmate. He didn't know why his thoughts jumped to that ending for his cellmate rather than him getting out. He guessed that was just the way his mind worked.

He approached the bunk and threw his scant belongings up onto the thin mattress. Other people would have brought their own things in with them, photos of loved ones, children or girlfriends or wives. Nicholas didn't have any of those people in his life. He was completely alone. When he'd been checked into reception, he'd been issued some basic toiletries, a toothbrush, and toilet roll. He'd also been given a set of sheets with which to make his bed, but a deep weariness had settled into his bones. What did he care if he was going to sleep on an unmade bed? It was the last of his concerns right now.

"Aren't you gonna ask me what my name is?" his new cellmate said. "I asked yours."

Nicholas pulled himself up onto the bunk and then lay flat on his back, staring at the ceiling. An underlying stench of body odour and damp rose from the mattress. The white paint was lined with numerous cracks, and when he let his gaze travel farther down to where the ceiling became the wall, he saw someone had scraped the outline of a balls and cock.

"Well, aren't you?"

Nicholas jumped at the other man's voice. For a moment, he'd completely forgotten he wasn't alone.

"What's your name?" he asked reluctantly. He didn't really give a shit what his cellmate was called.

The man below him snorted. "Everyone calls me Fish."

Nicholas kept his eyes on the ceiling. "Fish?"

"Yeah, 'cause I'm as slippery as one."

"Isn't that supposed to be eels?"

This conversation was confusing him. People didn't have names like Fish or Eel. He could already tell he wasn't going to do well in this place. Being a loner, like he was, wasn't a good thing. He needed to have a gang mentality to make friends and fit in, but that had never been his way.

His thoughts went to the detective who was behind him being here. It was her fault everything had gone wrong in his life. She hadn't saved his brother when she'd had the chance, and then she'd ruined everything by getting her police friends involved and having him put here. At least he'd managed to take her husband from her before that happened. Though only a small kernel of satisfaction, it kept him warm at night when the despair tried to creep into his soul.

An eye for an eye.

He'd played that moment in his head time and time again, the sudden shock and finality when he pushed the husband in front of the Tube train, and her scream as she'd realised what he'd done. He'd wanted to add her eyes to the collection of those who'd come before her, the ones who'd underestimated him, and she'd denied him that. Maybe he'd have let her live. She'd have had to find her way in the world blind, and with no husband. Her career would have been over, too. All she'd have had left was her daughter, but he didn't want to punish the kid. Children were always the innocents in these situations.

He'd known it well enough from when he'd been growing up. His own mother had been an uncaring bitch, just like that detective.

Nicholas didn't get much time to rest. Before he knew it, the buzzers were sounding again, and the metal door opened.

"You came on the right day," Fish declared, hopping to his feet. "It's chip night. Everyone gets excited for chip night."

Nicholas didn't have much of an appetite right now, but he needed to join in and make himself a part of the prison community. What he really wanted was to stay lying on the bunk, staring at the ceiling, lost in thought so he could forget where he was, but doing so would signal him as a weirdo, and people who were different didn't do well in life, never mind in prison.

Fish—or Eel, whatever his name was—showed him the ropes, taking him down to the canteen where they lined up for food to be dumped onto a plastic tray. Male bodies of all shapes, sizes, and skin tones packed the dining hall. Many were scrawled with tattoos—even the older ones. They all wore the same prison uniform and hard expressions. Their low conversation filled the air, together with the stink of boiled cabbage and the tang of bleach. It was impossible for Nicholas not to feel intimidated by them all, and he was thankful his cellmate—no matter how annoying his laugh might be—had taken him under his wing. Everyone seemed to know each other and headed to various groups and free spots at the tables. Nicholas was propelled back to his days at school where he'd never known where to sit at lunchtime.

Fish jabbed an elbow into his side. "Don't just stand there. This way."

He jerked his head, telling Nicholas to follow him over to one of the tables. A few prisoners were already there, shovelling their meals into their mouths. A couple of them glanced up with vague interest at Nicholas as Fish plonked his tray down into one of the empty spaces and then motioned for Nicholas to sit next to him.

The biggest of the men narrowed his eyes at Nicholas. "Who the fuck is this?"

"Hey, Rocko," Fish started, his voice heightened by nerves or excitement, "this is Nicholas Bailey, the bloke who pushed that detective's husband in front of a Tube train. Remember him?"

Rocko was a thick mass of muscle, topped by a shaved head. He was probably twice Nicholas's bodyweight. He eyed Nicholas suspiciously for a moment and then lifted his chin. "Yeah, I remember. Shame it wasn't the detective instead, though, am I right?"

"They caught me before I managed it," he muttered.

"Yeah? How did it feel, though, pushing that man in front of a train? Tell us everything."

A ball of pride swelled in Nicholas's chest. These men were showing him interest and respect. For once in his life, he wasn't being mocked or ignored. Could it be that they were more like him than he'd first thought, that maybe he'd finally found people who would understand him? His whole life, he'd been on the outskirts of everything, overlooked by everyone. He'd never known how to properly interact with other people and had watched others do with such ease that he seemed to find impossible. His brother had been the only one he'd ever really known how to talk to. He had never made Nicholas feel stupid or awkward or dumb. Maybe these people would be like his brother had been to him.

It was wrong to have hope in a place like this, but Nicholas couldn't help himself. As more of the prisoners gathered around, he talked, recounting all the terrible things he'd done, elaborating when they asked for more detail, giving them what they wanted. One of the officers came near, and he dropped his voice, and one of the other men started talking about something completely different. The officer walked away again, and Nicholas received a nudge in the ribs to tell him to keep going.

"You're all right, Bailey," Rocko said, nodding, his lower lip jutted out. "You know that? You'll fit right in."

Nicholas's heart expanded with happiness.

Chapter Four

Erica's shoes squeaked on the hospital flooring, the stink of cleaning products and illness assaulting her nostrils. As much as she loved her job, if there was one thing she could change, it would be the amount of time she ended up spending in hospitals.

She'd got a call from PC Dailey, the uniformed officer who'd gone in the ambulance with the victim, to say Brandon Skehan was out of surgery. Erica had done a background check on the victim, but he didn't have a record, and hadn't been the victim of any crimes in the past—at least none that he'd reported. She wanted to speak to Skehan as soon as possible to get his version of events. It was almost three a.m., and she'd been tempted to grab a few hours' sleep and see him in the morning, but this couldn't wait. They were on the hunt for a man who had attacked someone with a knife, and for all they knew, this might not be an isolated incident. If the victim had any information which could help them catch who did this before they hurt someone else, Erica didn't have time to sleep.

The uniformed officer sat outside the hospital room door. He was a young man, in his twenties, and he spotted Erica and jumped to his feet.

"DI Swift," she introduced herself. "How's the patient?"

"He's conscious, since they didn't need to put him under fully. I believe they just gave him a local anaesthetic rather than a general one. But he's been given some strong painkillers, and he's been sleeping. The doctors said the surgery went well. He was very lucky he didn't lose his eye, but he's going to have some impressive scarring. I believe they're going to have a plastic surgeon speak to him about further surgeries that will improve its appearance later down the line."

"Has he spoken at all?"

PC Dailey shook his head. "Nothing of any significance. He asked for some water, that's about it."

"What about in the ambulance? Did he say anything then?"

"Only that someone attacked him, and he was pretty convinced it was a man, but he didn't know who it was. He kept asking why someone would do this to him, so I assume he doesn't know the reason behind it either. He was very afraid that he'd lose his sight and at that point the paramedics were unable to get a good look at his injuries because there was so much blood."

Erica blew out a breath. "Jesus, poor bloke. It must have been terrifying."

"I managed to get some photographs of his injuries before he was taken for surgery. I've uploaded them for you to access."

"Great, thanks. I'll go and see if I can have a word with him. Feel free to go and grab yourself a coffee, if you want to."

Dailey offered her a smile. "Thanks, I will, though the coffee here is nothing to write home about. At least it's got caffeine."

She waited until Dailey had walked off down the corridor, and then she knocked lightly on the hospital room door and opened it. A figure lay in the bed under some low lighting. A machine pumped fluids into the drips that ran into the veins on his arm.

The man in the bed had half his face wrapped in white bandages. The other eye was closed, his dark lashes—the same jet black as the thick crop of hair on his head—resting on his cheek. He had a strong build, though his lower half was covered with the hospital sheet and his upper with the less-than-attractive hospital nightgown.

"Mr Skehan," she said softly as she walked in. "Are you awake? I'm DI Swift, and I need to ask you a few questions about what happened to you."

The man moaned softly and twisted his head against the pillow. She felt bad that she was trying to wake him up when he clearly needed to rest and heal, but it was important that she at least try to speak to him. If he had any idea who'd done this to him, she needed to know. Right now, there was a dangerous man still at large in the community.

She crossed the room and stopped at his bedside. "Mr Skehan." She spoke louder this time. "I really need to talk to you."

His remaining good eye fluttered open, revealing a dark-blue iris. He stared up at her, confused for a moment, and then tried to sit up.

"It's okay, Mr Skehan. You don't have to sit up. Stay right where you are."

He groaned and turned his face away. "I'm sleeping." His speech was slurred, and he was hard to understand.

"I know you're tired, but I really need to ask you some questions about what happened tonight. Do you think you could do that for me?"

He muttered something unintelligible, and his eye slipped shut again.

Erica clenched her hands into fists. "Mr Skehan? Please, could you wake up for a moment so I can speak to you?"

She had the feeling this wasn't going to go anywhere and bit down on her frustration. He'd told the uniformed officer that he hadn't known the person who'd attacked him, and she doubted he'd tell her any differently now. He might have been able to give her a description though, which could have narrowed things down. At the moment, they didn't have a whole lot to go on. She just hoped whoever had done this had been stupid enough to leave prints on the handle of the knife, and that they'd be able to match them to some they had on record.

Movement came at the door, and she turned, half expecting to see the police officer back with his coffee, but instead a different man, this one in a white coat, entered the room.

"Your colleague said you were in here," the man said. "I'm Doctor Burkhart, I'm taking care of Mr Skehan."

"Right." She took a step back from the bed. "I'm DI Swift. How's he getting on?"

"I'm sorry, Detective, but he's really not in any fit state to answer any questions right now. While we didn't give him a general anaesthetic when we stitched him up, he was given a light sedative before we gave him the local injections. It's highly unlikely you'll get any sense out of him, and he most likely won't remember any of this in the morning."

"I understand, but I had to try. It's an important part of my job to get a statement from the victim."

The doctor came farther into the room and offered her a smile that didn't quite reach his eyes. "And it's an important part of mine to make sure a patient gets enough rest so he can heal properly."

"Understood. Is it all right if I come back in the morning?"

"Make it mid-morning. The sedatives will have worn off by then, and you'll be far more likely to get a proper statement from him."

"No problem. I suppose I'll just have to hope whoever did this to him doesn't decide to attack another innocent person in the meantime."

He didn't even flinch at her jibe. "I'm sure you have other ways of catching the bad guy, Detective."

"Absolutely." She turned for the door but was still annoyed that she hadn't managed to speak to the victim herself. Then she stopped. "Before I go, can I just ask how well you'll think he'll heal?"

"Physically, he'll heal well enough. He's going to have most problems with the eyelid that was slashed. We've stitched it back together, but when it heals it's going to feel tight, and he'll probably feel as though he won't be able to close it properly, and he may well deal with some dry eye issues. Mentally, he'll most likely take a little longer to get over what's happened to him. He was lucky not to have lost that eye."

"So I hear. Thank you for your time, Doctor."

She left the room. The officer had made it back and was nursing a cup of something hot and steaming. "Let me know if there are any changes," she said.

He nodded. "Will do."

Erica checked her watch. It was approaching four a.m. which meant she was only going to get a few hours' sleep now, but if she was going to get even that, she needed to go home and get her head down.

She'd come back in the morning.

Chapter Five

Erica suppressed a yawn behind the back of her hand and blinked tired, gritty eyes. She'd managed to grab a couple of hours of sleep between leaving the hospital and coming back into work again, but it hadn't been anywhere near enough. She was already on to her second cup of coffee and thought she was going to need even more if she was going to stay focused.

She'd placed a quick call to the hospital to check how Brandon Skehan had got on overnight, and been told that he was stable. She pulled up the photographs the uniformed officer had uploaded to the evidence file and grimaced. He'd also uploaded the video from his body-worn video camera, but it wasn't as clear as the photographs he'd taken on his work mobile. The video did, however, show the distress the victim had been in when they'd arrived. He was kneeling on the pavement with both hands over his face and blood pouring between his fingers. The attending officers on-scene attempted to calm him and let them look at his wounds, but he just kept shouting about the man in the flat. Erica assumed he was talking about his attacker. Only moments after, the ambulance arrived and paramedics took over. The uniformed officer had the good sense to take a couple of photos on his mobile before the paramedics covered the wound with compressions to try to stem the bleeding.

The photographs did not make for pleasant viewing. The cut ran horizontally across the right side of his face, starting at the inside of his nose and drawing it over his eyelid, towards his right ear. It appeared to have been done in one slash, rather than a series of stabbing or hacking movements. The amount of blood the wound had caused made it difficult to see too much detail, but a part of the eyelid appeared to be hanging down in a flap.

Who would do such a thing to another person completely unprovoked?

She'd covered cases where people had done far worse to total strangers. There was no limit to how awful the human race could be to one another at times.

"I see Acting DS Rudd isn't in yet," DC Howard said, pushing a cup of coffee across Erica's desk towards her. "Shouldn't we be starting a briefing soon? Surely the Acting DS should be present?"

"Thank you for your concern, Howard, but neither of us got back home much before four a.m., and considering it's only just gone nine now, I think we can give her a few more minutes."

"You got to bed at the same time she did, but you managed to get into work on time."

She put down her pen and gave him a tight smile. "I'm the boss. I need to be here. I'd rather Rudd got a few more minutes' shuteye and was on her best form this morning than if she came back into work exhausted." *Like I am,* she thought but didn't say. She hadn't even managed to see Poppy that morning. Since she'd been out all night, Poppy had slept over at Natasha's house. Erica would have liked to take her to school, but that would have meant losing even more sleep, and Natasha had told her not to be silly, she was more than happy to take Poppy in with her cousins. The other parents at school—and probably a few of the teachers, too—must think that Natasha was Poppy's mother. There were times when Erica picked Poppy up or dropped her off where she was sure people were looking at her, wondering who she was. She was never going to be one of those mothers who home baked cakes for a bake sale or handmade costumes for World Book Day. The best she could manage was throwing some money at the school every now and then. She hoped Poppy wouldn't resent her for it in years to come. She also wished she could be one of those people who didn't care what other people thought of her, but it seemed that button was broken.

"If there's anything you need me to do to fill in while she's still getting her beauty sleep," Howard continued, "just let me know."

"I'm sure you've got plenty of your own work to get on with," she replied curtly.

He pursed his lips but nodded and went back to his own desk.

Erica understood full well what DC Howard was doing. He hadn't been happy that she hadn't picked him to be Acting DS while Shawn was on annual leave. Shawn would be back tomorrow, thank God. DC Howard moping around the office like a sulky child had been irritating. She didn't know why he did it. All it did was ensure she was even less likely to choose him when the time came again.

She'd heard rumours about how it had been some kind of reverse sexism, and she'd only chosen Hannah Rudd because she was another woman, and if it had been down to DCI Gibbs to do the picking, he was sure to have chosen Howard. Erica knew this wasn't the case. It was Howard's slightly cocky behaviour that meant he hadn't been chosen, and she knew

Gibbs had noticed it as well. Hannah Rudd did the work; she didn't make a show and dance over it.

As though Erica's thoughts had conjured her, Rudd rushed in, her cheeks flushed.

"Sorry I'm late, boss. I got a call that one of the houses a couple down from the one with the dog has security cameras. They had a break-in twelve months ago and have been paranoid about it since. I swung by on my way here to pick up the footage. I figured it might be important."

Erica did her best not to throw a challenging look in DC Howard's direction, wondering what he would have to say about that.

"That's excellent," Erica said, giving her Acting DS a smile. "Assuming the assailant went that way, we should catch him on camera."

"That's what I'm hoping, too. I managed to speak to some of the other neighbours while you were at the hospital as well, but so far none of them saw anything other than the aftermath of the attack, when the shouting started, and we showed up."

"Whoever did this was slippery enough. Considering the houses are all backing onto each other on that street, you'd have thought someone would have noticed a strange man nipping through their back garden in the middle of the night."

She shrugged. "It was late, and people were asleep."

"This is London. People are always awake, and we need something to go on."

"Hopefully, the victim will be able to tell us something about his attacker. Maybe he even knows who it was but is covering for them."

"Perhaps," Erica arched a brow, "though if someone had done that to my face, I don't think I'd cover for them. We need to find out a little more about Brandon Skehan, though. What sort of things is he into? Who are his family and friends? What does his boss and colleagues think of him? Do any of them know of anyone who might want to hurt him?"

"I can look into that," she offered.

Erica shook her head. "No, you're busy with the neighbours. Delegate that job to DC Howard."

"Will do."

Howard wasn't going to like Rudd telling him what to do, and she expected Rudd was going to feel awkward doing the telling. But part of climbing the ranks meant being able to delegate work—as much as Erica wanted to do everything all the time, it simply wasn't possible, and that was what teamwork was all about. It was good for Howard to learn a bit of humility and for Rudd to be more assertive.

With everyone in, she called a briefing to bring them up to speed with what had happened overnight. Gibbs sat in on the meeting, but other than saying good morning, he remained at the back and let Erica take the lead.

DCI Gibbs had returned to work a few months earlier, and Erica had been happy to hand both the reins and the job title back to him. She'd come to the conclusion that she didn't need the extra responsibility right now, or the extra paperwork, of being a DCI, Acting or otherwise. Gibbs had mostly recovered from the stroke, but when it got late in the day, he grew weaker down one side of his body, and she noted how that same side of his face seemed to droop. He clearly had some ongoing issues, but they hadn't been enough to prevent him from returning to work, something both he, and his wife, had clearly been happy about. "If I had to spend another day watching crappy daytime television, I would have given myself another stroke," he'd told her not long after he'd got back into the office. "Longest month of my life."

Erica went through the roll call and got started.

"Good morning, everyone. At approximately eleven-thirty last night, twenty-nine-year-old Brandon Skehan was attacked in his home with a knife. We believe the attacker to be male, but other than that, we have no further description of the assailant." She brought up photographs of Brandon Skehan's injuries. "The attacker left the weapon at the scene, and it's currently being processed by forensics." She clicked the computer to show an aerial view of the rows of houses. "We believe the assailant both entered and escaped from the rear of the property, which means he must have gone over the back wall or fences until he reached one of the alleyways that lead back onto the road here," she pointed out one of the access points, "or here, or here. We don't yet know if he was on foot or in a car, but we have some CCTV footage from a neighbouring house security camera that will hopefully catch him." She took a few paces across the front of the room and came to a halt again. "As of yet, we have no motive for the crime. Nothing was stolen, that we're aware of. I'm going to speak to the victim at the hospital, but I also want us to find out everything we can about Brandon Skehan. Someone out there decided to do this to him, and I want to know why."

Erica made sure everyone knew what their actions were for that day and then drew the meeting to a close.

She had some paperwork from a previous case to catch up on, and then she'd go back to the hospital and speak to the victim. She also hoped forensics would send a report through quickly. There was nothing worse than having a case with no decent leads. It always left her floundering. Shawn would be landing in the UK later that day. She hoped he'd had a good holiday, but she was looking forward to having him back in the office. It never felt right when one of her team weren't in.

• • • •

ERICA CALLED AHEAD this time to make sure she'd be able to speak to Brandon Skehan and then she drove to the hospital and walked up to the ward.

The doctor who'd chastised her during the early hours stood at the ward's reception desk, his head bent over a file.

"You're still working, I see," she said, drawing his attention away from the clipboard.

He checked his watch. "I'm finishing shortly. I'll be in again tonight."

"I see. And how is Mr Skehan this morning?"

"He's doing well. He's still on some strong pain medication, but he's awake and talking."

"That's good. I assume it's okay if I go and have a word with him now?"

"Yes, that's fine, and, Detective, I really do hope you find whoever did this."

"We're doing our best."

Brandon Skehan was awake when she entered the room. A television was on in the corner, but someone had put it on mute, so only the picture served as entertainment.

"Mr Skehan," she said as she moved into his line of sight. "I'm DI Swift. I came to see you in the early hours to try and ask you some questions, but you were still recovering from the surgery. Do you remember?"

He frowned in her direction. "No, sorry. I don't."

She flashed him a smile. "Well, you seem a bit brighter now. Are you feeling up to having a chat about what happened to you?"

He fixed his remaining good eye on her and nodded. "I thought someone would be around to talk to me. On top of being attacked, one of your lot stole my clothes."

He didn't sound pissed off about it, his tone surprisingly jovial, considering everything he'd gone through. It was helped by the soft lilt of an Irish accent, and some heavy-duty painkillers.

She crossed the room and pulled up a chair beside the bed and sat down in it. "Sorry about that. They were needed as evidence. We might be able to get the attacker's blood from them if he was injured in the struggle."

"Then you'll have to excuse the fetching outfit." He threw her a disarming smile. "I'm not looking my best."

She sat back and crossed her legs. "Don't worry about that. I've seen a lot worse."

"That's not exactly a compliment." He pushed himself to sit upright on the bed and winced.

"Is there anything I can do to help you?" she offered. "Can I get you a nurse?"

"No, I'm fine. Just stiff and sore after..." He waved his hand in the direction of his face.

"Of course. That's completely understandable, Mr Skehan."

"My name's Brandon. Mr Skehan makes me sound like my dad."

She smiled at that. "You don't sound as though you're from around here?"

"No, I'm not. I'm from Belfast, but I've been here for ten years, much to my mother's dismay. She's always said that London was a dangerous place."

And Belfast isn't? Erica thought but didn't say.

"And now you're going to have a pretty impressive scar with which she can make her point."

"Aye, exactly. The plastic surgeon came around and talked to me, though, and said the scar shouldn't be too bad. They did everything they could to minimise the damage. He also said women normally have a thing for scars, so it might not be all bad."

"Well, I don't know about that, but I'm glad there was no permanent damage to your sight."

"Me, too. It was what I was most worried about. Well, that and some feckin' psycho trying to kill me."

"That's why I'm here, Brandon. I want to find the person who did this to you."

"You mean you haven't caught him yet?"

"No, I'm sorry. By the time we arrived at the scene, he'd already run, but it's my job to find violent criminals, and I'll do everything I can to track him down. I will need a little help from you, though."

"Aye, sure. I'll do whatever I can to help. I don't much like the idea of going home, knowing that bastard was in my house."

"Do you have any idea of who might have done this? Anyone you've fallen out with recently?"

He shook his head. "No, I've not a clue. Just because I'm Irish doesn't mean I like to brawl or anything."

She shifted in her seat. "I didn't think that. It's the first question I'd ask of anybody in this situation."

"Ah, right. I wondered if it might have been because I was Irish, though. Maybe someone out there doesn't like us much."

"It's still early days, so we'll keep all possibilities open. Do you live alone?"

"Yes, I do. Haven't quite managed to find someone who'll put up with me enough to want to live with me yet."

He threw her that half smile again.

"No children then?" she checked.

"Not that I know of."

"And how long have you been at that address?"

"Not long." He shrugged. "Less than a year."

"What about your spare time? How do you like to spend it?"

"I don't have any hobbies or anything like that, if that's what you mean. I hang out with friends, go to the pub, watch films on Netflix and that sort of thing."

"What were you doing before the attack?"

"Exactly that. I'd been having a couple of drinks with some mates down at the pub, and that son of a bitch must have been lying in wait for me or something. It was dark, and I didn't even manage to put on the hallway light. I threw my keys onto the side and was pulling off my jacket when he attacked."

Erica made a note to speak to those friends in case any of them saw anyone unusual hanging around and also to get the CCTV from the pub.

"Do you think he was alone?" she asked.

"As far as I know, but I can't say for certain."

"Do you think you might have interrupted a burglary?"

He fixed her with his one good eye. "You tell me? Did it look as though the flat had been gone through?"

"At first glance, it's hard to tell. Of course, it's difficult for us to tell if something was missing or not, but nothing big had been taken. The expensive items like the television and your laptop were still there. Once you get home, perhaps you'll be able to check through the drawers and see if anything smaller is missing."

"I can do that. Like I said, whatever it takes to find the guy."

Erica settled back in her seat. "Tell me about what happened preceding the attack. Start from when you got up that morning."

He sighed and lifted his gaze to the ceiling. "I got up about seven-thirty and got ready for work."

"What do you do for a job?"

"I work on the security desk at Canada Square in Canary Wharf."

"And you went straight into work? How do you get there?"

He shrugged. "I just get the Tube and then change to the Docklands Light Rail. The station is about ten minutes from my front door, so it's convenient."

"And did anything unusual happen at work? Did you have any run-ins with anyone? Prevented someone from entering the building or thrown someone out?"

He gave a small laugh. "It's not like I'm a bouncer in a nightclub. I deal with people in suits all day. They tend not to cause much trouble."

"You didn't notice anyone unusual lurking outside or anything like that? Nobody caught your attention."

He frowned and sat forward slightly. "You think they might have followed me from work."

Erica gestured with both hands. "Again, at this point, it's a case of making sure we've covered all possibilities."

"I understand, but no, I didn't notice anything or anyone strange. It was just a normal day...right until it wasn't."

Erica sat back. "Did you go straight home after work?"

"Aye, I grabbed a shower and got changed, and then headed back out again."

"What about dinner? Did you eat while you were out?"

"I thought I'd probably get a kebab at some point. Can't beat a good kebab and chips after a few pints."

She tilted her head, questioningly. "And did you?"

"No." He laughed again. "I filled up on the pints."

Erica nodded. "I'm going to need a list of everywhere you went and the approximate times. If someone was watching you, a security camera might have caught them. I'm also going to need the names of the friends you were out with that night."

"But if you don't know who it was, how will you know who to look for?"

He had a point.

"It'll help us build our case. What time would you say you got back home?"

He thought for a moment. "About eleven-thirty. I opened my front door, chucked my keys on the side. The flat was in darkness, but that's normal. I was planning just to go straight to bed and pass out."

"What happened after you threw your keys on the side?"

"I walked down the hall planning to go to my bedroom. I must have heard a noise, but I'm not sure what—maybe the scrape of a foot, or just someone breathing—but it stopped me walking. I felt myself do that freeze thing, you know, when your body goes stiff and you're straining your ears, and literally, a second later, movement darted out at me, and a knife slashed my face, right across my eyes. Thank fuck I managed to jerk back a wee bit, so it only did the damage it did, 'cause I think the bastard would have cut me bad otherwise. I'm lucky I still have my eyes."

Erica shuddered at the mental image. She'd worked on a case previously where the victims hadn't been so lucky. "And then what did you do?"

"I lashed out at the knife and I must have knocked it from his grip, 'cause it fell to the floor."

"You saw it?"

He shook his head. "No, I heard it. It clattered when he dropped it." He gave a soft snort of laughter. "I wish I could tell you that I throat-chopped the attacker and did a cool kick to take his legs out from under him, but I didn't do any of that."

"I wouldn't have expected you to," she said. She liked people who were able to keep a sense of humour about them over such frightening circumstance.

Brandon continued. "I couldn't see anything, partly 'cause it was dark, but also because my eyes were filled with blood. I was lucky that I was facing my front door 'cause I bravely ran away. I put my hands out, and even though I couldn't see a fucking thing, I ran for the front door. I remembered shouting for help, but it was late, and I had no idea if anyone was around to hear me. I must have moved faster than I thought, 'cause adrenaline was just pouring into me, and I somehow managed to open the front door and get out onto the road."

"Whoever attacked you didn't chase after you?"

"No. I mean, I don't think so. I couldn't see anything, so maybe he did, but then saw that woman who came to help me and ran off." He glanced away. "I'm just guessing, though. I couldn't see a thing."

"Do you think he left via the rear of your flat?"

"I suppose so. Maybe he even got in that way. I have no idea." He paused and then asked, "Do you like your job, Detective?"

The question surprised her. "Yes, I do. I love it."

"I'd considered getting into the police force myself years ago, after I finished school. But then I got distracted by partying and just wanted to have a good time for a few years, and it never happened."

"There's still time. Plenty of people don't start until their twenties."

He gave that half-smile. "I'm six months off thirty."

Erica laughed. "That still counts. If it's something you're serious about, the Met could always do with more officers, especially good ones. If you have a background in security, you might make a good candidate."

"And then I could help prevent someone doing this," he gestured to his face, "to another person."

"That's one of the main reasons I love my job," she admitted. "I hate to see decent, law-abiding citizens being affected by the illegal acts of others. Sometimes it feels like the world is a very unfair place, but it helps to feel as though I'm rebalancing the scales a little bit."

She thought to Chris and what her family had been through. They'd never done anything to bring such horror upon them—she'd literally been in the wrong place at the wrong time when Nicholas Bailey's brother had died—and yet they'd all been punished severely for it. Now Bailey would be spending the rest of his life behind bars as his punishment. Did the two equal out? She didn't think so, but it was a form of justice, at least. Would the man lying in the hospital bed in front of her think whatever sentence his attacker would eventually receive be enough to payback the scars he'd now be forced to live with?

Brandon gave her a cautious smile, as though he could read what was going through her mind. "I like that idea."

A nurse knocked on the door and stuck her head into the room. "Sorry, check-up time."

Erica rose to her feet. "That's okay, I'm done here." She plucked one of her cards from her jacket pocket and placed it on the small over-the-bed table that also held some of Brandon Skehan's belongings. "If you think of anything else that might help us find who did that to you, please, don't hesitate to call."

"Aye, I won't. I'll be happy to call you, Detective." He finished with another smile.

Her stomach flipped. Was he flirting with her? There had been an easy camaraderie between them the whole time, something that was surprising considering the circumstances. Besides, it didn't mean anything. He had that Irish charm and was probably like it with everyone.

The nurse swept into the room, pushing a trolley containing additional bottles for his drips. "How are you feeling?"

"All the better for seeing you," he quipped and threw Erica a wink with his one good eye, which didn't quite give the effect he'd probably been hoping for.

She found herself smiling, though. She'd been right in thinking that was just his personality.

She slipped out of the room. It was disappointing that he hadn't been able to give her any leads on who had done this to him, but at least he was going to be okay. She was going to have to hope Rudd had got on better with the neighbours and the CCTV, and that one of them had seen something. She also had the report from SOCO on its way. With any luck, the attacker wouldn't have been wearing any gloves and they'd be able to pick some prints from the handle.

Luck wasn't something she could rely on, though. Good police work always trumped good fortune.

Chapter Six

Erica grabbed a sandwich and a coffee on the way back into the office and sat at her desk to eat. In between mouthfuls, she phoned DC Howard and gave him the names of the men Brandon Skehan said he'd been out with before the attack, and also the name of the pub where they'd been drinking. Howard had already been looking into Skehan's family and friends, so it made sense for him to do it.

The forensic report from the flat and the garden were back, and she opened them up with interest, a flickering of hope in her chest that this would give them a decent lead.

She read through it, her brow drawing into a frown, that flicker of hope doused like a bucket of water over a campfire.

She picked up the phone and dialled Keith Allen, who was a Forensic Submissions Officer.

"Hi, it's DI Swift. I've just gone through the report on the Skehan case. Tell me it isn't right."

"Hang on a sec. Let me just pull it up." There was a pause and the distant tapping of fingers on a keyboard. "Okay, shoot."

"Forensics didn't get anything from the crime scene, and I'm finding that hard to believe. I get that there might not be prints on the knife or prints on the door anywhere, other than that of the victim, but the rest of it doesn't seem right. Blood spatters, hair, and clothing fibres were all matched to the victim. Assuming the assailant went over the top of the wall, which, other than the fences either side, would have been his only escape route, I'd have expected to at least find clothing fibres caught in the brickwork, but there was nothing."

"Perhaps the assailant was wearing protective clothing," Allen said.

"Maybe, but there were no signs of anyone having jumped down, either. We've had rain recently, and there was a flowerbed, which was mostly just dirt, directly on the other side, but we didn't find any shoe prints at all."

"Could he have jumped farther, out onto the grass, so he avoided the mud?"

Erica fiddled with a pen and scribbled with force onto a piece of paper. "A possibility, yes, though I'd have been amazed he avoided all the dog mess—there were no footprints in that either."

"Maybe he didn't jump down there. He might have crawled or walked along the wall and got down into a different garden."

"Again, possibly, but I'd still expect to find clothing fibres. Those fences weren't strong enough to hold a man's weight, so he must have pulled himself up onto the wall, and the chances of not leaving anything are zero."

"You're saying he didn't get onto the wall?"

"If he did, he was naked and somehow has the ability not to sweat or shed skin or hair either."

She blew out her cheeks. Was she wrong about him going over the wall? She'd checked the two fences either side of the small backyard, and there was no way someone would have been able to scale them without them collapsing. She was going to need to go back to the crime scene and reassess her assumptions, though she couldn't see how he would have gone any other way. But the dog in the house behind hadn't barked either, which also suggested her instinct about him going over the wall had been wrong.

She tried not to give in to her frustrations. Other than the attacker being male—and even that wasn't one hundred percent certain—they had very little to go on. Everything she thought would produce a lead had ended up being a dead end.

"Okay, thanks for your help, Keith."

"Sorry I couldn't help more."

She ended the call but barely had time to put her thoughts together before Hannah Rudd approached her desk.

"Sorry, boss. I've gone through the neighbour's security footage from several hours before the attack to several hours after, and I can't see anyone on it."

"Shit." Erica thought for a moment. "If the camera didn't catch anything, and there's no route out from the back gardens between the houses, it means our guy went in the other direction. It's not what we wanted, but it helps narrow down what his actions were after fleeing the scene."

"We've gathered all the car registrations from around that area," Rudd said, "so we can make sure there were no unusual vehicles around at the time?"

"Good. Let me know if that produces anything."

Rudd nodded and left, just as Howard arrived. The two of them passed without acknowledging each other, and Erica pursed her lips. She hoped Howard wasn't going to keep causing friction in the office.

"Thought you'd want an update," Howard said as he stopped in front of her desk. "I was able to track down the two friends Skehan met up with the evening of his attack. They both describe themselves as his colleagues rather than friends and said they haven't known him long. But I checked out the CCTV of the pub they went to, and they were all there together drinking, not heavily, by the looks of it, just a couple of pints. They said Skehan made his excuses about eleven and headed home, while they stayed out and went to a club."

Erica frowned. "Is that normal? For him to go home and them to go on somewhere else, I mean?"

"I asked the same question, and they said they didn't know Skehan well enough to be able to say what he normally would or wouldn't do. They said he's a bit of a loner and that he didn't have many mates."

"He's not from London. Shame he's not managed to fit in, though. He seems like a friendly enough bloke."

Howard shrugged. "It's different for men. We don't make friends in the same way you women do. Beer and football is about all we tend to have in common."

"What about the CCTV footage from the pub and the surrounding area?" she asked. "Did it capture anyone suspicious? Anyone following Skehan to the Tube station?"

"Nope, nothing like that. They just looked like a group of blokes on a night out. No one around set any alarm bells ringing, and the pub landlord didn't see anyone suspicious hanging around either. Skehan didn't get into any arguments or fights, that the landlord had noticed. He said it was just a normal night out."

Erica huffed out a breath. "That doesn't help us any."

When were they going to get a break on this case?

. . . .

ERICA STOPPED BY BRANDON Skehan's flat on the way to pick Poppy up from Natasha's. She'd worked far too many hours over the past day or two and she needed an evening with her daughter and a decent night's sleep. She wouldn't be able to catch Brandon Skehan's attacker if she was exhausted and couldn't think straight. She knew her own limits, and while she could miss one night of sleep and still function like a human being, two nights was pushing it.

She did her best to take in the property with fresh eyes, trying to figure out where the attacker might have escaped from if he hadn't gone over that back wall. With Brendon and the witnesses all gathered out the front while the emergency services were called, there was no way he could have escaped from the front of the property without being seen. That meant he either went out the back, or he hid inside the building until everyone had gone. Could he have gone to the upstairs' neighbour's flat? The property had been checked, but maybe they'd missed something. What if Julie Luxford had been hiding something, or someone? Erica made a mental note to speak to the other woman again.

Feeling as though she wasn't getting anywhere, she left for Natasha's.

She wasn't the only one to be happy about spending a night at home. When she arrived to pick up her daughter, Poppy flung her arms around her waist.

"What do you want for dinner tonight?" Erica asked her. She couldn't remember the last time she'd actually managed to do a decent supermarket shop. She only ever seemed to have time to grab the basics from the local Tesco Express.

"Fish and chips," Poppy declared.

It would save her cooking—and shopping for whatever it was she thought she might cook—though it was hardly the healthiest of meals. But now Poppy had suggested it, Erica couldn't imagine eating anything else, and she convinced herself that they both deserved a treat.

"That sounds like a very good idea. Let's swing by the chip shop on the way home."

They got home clutching paper-wrapped bundles of salt-and-vinegar-steaming fish and chips, and ate it on their laps in front of the television. Erica kept an eye on her phone for any developments on the case, but right now she had the feeling it was going to go cold. There was nothing more frustrating than a case she couldn't solve. They happened, of course they did, but she preferred it when they didn't.

With greasy fingers and full stomachs, Erica bundled the leftovers back into the paper and shoved them in the bin.

"Can I have ice cream?" Poppy called from the other room.

"Let your dinner go down first or you'll get sick."

The doorbell chimed through the house. Who was that? It was almost seven and time for Poppy's bath and bedtime. She wiped her hands on a tea towel and went to answer it.

The shape through the glass panel in the front door cut a familiar figure.

A grin spread across Erica's face as she opened it. "Hello, stranger! You're back."

Shawn returned the smile. "Had to stop by and say hi to my two favourite people."

"It's good to have you back. How was the holiday?"

"Put it this way, I feel like I might need to go on a detox now. I think my blood may be ninety percent beer."

"That great a time, huh?"

He shrugged one shoulder. "Yeah, we had a few laughs. It got a little boring towards the end, though. Only so much sun and booze one man can take."

She realised she was leaving him standing on the doorstep and backed out of the way to let him into the hallway. "Sounds ideal to me."

"You should take Poppy away sometime. She'd love it."

Erica sighed and pushed her hand through her hair. "I keep playing with the idea. We used to go abroad when Chris was alive. The idea of doing it on my own just feels really weird."

She knew the possibility of Shawn offering to go with them hung on the air between them, but it wasn't as easy as that. For one, it would be near impossible for him to book annual leave at the same time as her. Secondly, it would be morally wrong, what with her being his boss. She could always try to find a new job role with a different department, but the thought of losing Shawn as her DS was even worse. When they were working together, she could rely on having him in her life. If they went down a different route, she might lose him as both a colleague and a friend. It simply wasn't worth the risk.

"You're going to need to get over that hurdle sometime, Erica. For Poppy's sake, as well as your own."

She risked a smile. "You mean I can't hide us both in the house forever?"

"No, you can't," he said sternly.

"I know. It's just not easy when you know what a dangerous place the world can be."

"Poppy couldn't ask for anyone better to keep her safe than you."

Erica sighed. "I wish I could believe you on that. Thing is, I didn't keep Chris safe, did I? Quite the opposite. If he'd never had me in his life, he'd still be alive."

"I'm sure he wouldn't have swapped a single day for not having you and Poppy."

Shawn was right. Chris had been a devoted father and husband. That was what made all of this even worse. She wasn't sure she'd ever get over the guilt and grief surrounding her loss of him. The idea of being able to move on and just get on with her life felt impossible.

"Anyway," he changed the tone, "I brought Poppy back a present."

"You did?"

"Yep." He reached into the carrier bag and pulled out a child-sized red flamenco dress, complete with frills, tassels, and black polka dots. "Ta-da."

"Oh my God. She's going to love it, thank you." Erica called over her shoulder. "Poppy, come here. Shawn's brought you a present."

She appeared in the lounge doorway. "A present?"

"Say hi to Shawn."

"Hi, Shawn. You got me a present?"

"Come here and speak to him properly," Erica chided.

The girl hurried over, and Shawn handed her the bag. She grinned and reached in to pull out the dress.

"It's like what all the Spanish girls wear at the horse festivals," he told her.

"See," Erica said, "you did get some culture."

"Can I try it on now?" Poppy asked.

Erica nodded. "Of course. Then come down and show us what it looks like."

She led Shawn into the kitchen and proceeded to put the kettle on.

"So, how's things been at work?" Shawn propped himself up against the worktop.

Erica took down a couple of mugs. "Busy. I'll be glad to have you back in. We need all the hands we can get right now. We've had a knife attack on a man in his twenties in his home, and as of yet, we don't have any suspects. He claims he can think of no reason why someone would have attacked him. He's lucky he didn't lose his eye. The frustrating thing is that I can't figure out how the attacker made his escape from the property. Forensics don't think he went over the back wall, and a light breeze would knock down the two fences either side of the property."

"Beamed into outer space by aliens?" Shawn suggested.

Erica chuckled. "I'm starting to think that might be the case."

"And how did Rudd get on with being Acting DS?"

"She's been great. Howard's had his arse in his hands over it all week, though. He clearly believes he should have been chosen over Rudd."

"That's Howard's issue, though," Shawn said. "He thinks he's a better detective than he is. Rudd just keeps her head down and gets on with whatever is thrown at her. Howard has a tendency to make a song and dance about things."

"I agree. He's just young, that's all. I think in another couple of years, when he's matured a little, he'll be the detective he wants to be. Men always seem to mature slower than women."

He grinned at her. "I hope you're not calling me immature."

"There are always exceptions," she teased.

Poppy burst into the room in a blur of red and black frills. She put both hands in the air and did a twirl. "Look how pretty it is."

"Look how pretty *you* are," Erica said, her heart warming at the sight of her daughter so happy.

Shawn was right. It wasn't fair on Poppy for Erica to keep her home simply because she was frightened of letting her out into the big wide world. After all, Chris had been home that day, and it hadn't kept him any safer. It was important for Poppy to experience a life outside of London. Maybe she could find somewhere quiet with sunshine and a bit of culture. She definitely didn't fancy going anywhere like the Costa del Sol, where it was full of British people getting drunk and eating the same terrible fried food they got at home, but there were plenty of other options. Yes, somewhere quiet where she and Poppy could spend some quality time together, swimming in the sea and building sandcastles and eating ice cream.

"Earth to Erica. You were miles away," Shawn said.

"I was. Just thinking that you were right about taking Poppy on holiday somewhere."

Poppy's eyes widened. "We're going on holiday? Like a proper holiday?"

"Hey, we've had proper holidays," Erica protested.

Poppy pouted and folded her arms. Erica got a flash of what her daughter would be like as a teen. "Mummy, we didn't even have a sleepover anywhere. I have more sleepovers with Aunty Tasha when you're working."

"Okay, I know, you're right. I've got some annual leave I need to take, but it won't happen for a few months yet, okay?"

"Yeah, that's okay."

Erica glanced up and caught Shawn's eye. He threw her a wink.

"Yes, okay, you were right," she conceded.

Poppy ran back off, and Erica finished making the tea.

Chapter Seven

Two Years Earlier

Nicholas was starting to get used to prison life, but that didn't mean he liked it.

Different smells permeated the air depending on the day. Fridays always meant Bombay potatoes, and the tang of spice mingled with boiled vegetables filtered through the whole jail.

Nicholas clutched the tray containing his food and turned towards the hall filled with prisoners. His gaze skirted across the multitude of heads, searching for a space where he could sit. This place was worse than school had been. Everyone had their own gang, and, despite his initial welcome, Nicholas hadn't found his own one.

He spotted the back of Fish's mostly bald head, and his stomach churned with a combination of relief and anxiety. At least he had something to aim for, instead of just standing there like an idiot with no direction.

He crossed the room, tray held out in front of him. Fish must have sensed him coming as he glanced up just as Nicholas reached him and rolled his eyes. Both of them clocked the space beside Fish, and instead of Fish nodding at it to let him know it was available, he slid sideways, filling it himself.

Fish forked up some of his curry and shoved it in his mouth before speaking.

"We share a cell, dude. It doesn't mean we're fucking married or something. You can sit somewhere else."

The men sitting around the table shot him looks that were a combination of amused, irritated, and plain hostile.

"Fine. Whatever."

Nicholas took a step back. His tray trembled, and he held it tighter and willed the shaking to stop. He recognised it as a result of the adrenaline flooding his system. His heartbeat was a heavy thump in his chest.

In his head he screamed, *fuck, fuck, fuuuucck.*

Outwardly, he just shrugged and turned away.

He didn't even want to eat his meal now, but he sensed all eyes on him, some of the other prisoners probably willing for a fight to break out so they had a little entertainment over lunch. He sensed his weakness radiate out from him and knew the men picked up on it.

A space at the end of one of the other tables opened up and, with relief, he sank into the empty spot. Farther down the table, five black men openly glared at him, and Nicholas prayed one of them wouldn't get to their feet and demand to know what he was doing sitting there.

Luckily, it seemed he wasn't worth their time, as they just shook their heads at him, sucked air in through their teeth, and went back to their conversation. Or perhaps there were too many officers around and they were waiting until they were in the exercise yard or even in the showers. Nicholas grew cold at the thought.

He'd completely lost his appetite, but he forced himself to shovel the curried potatoes into his mouth. Part of him was worried that if he didn't eat it, it would end up spilt into his lap or tipped over his head by one of the other inmates. He'd been such an idiot to think he might have found his people when he'd first arrived. Things were no different here to what they were on the outside. Inwardly, he squirmed at the recollection. He'd thought he was the big man, someone of importance. They'd encouraged him and asked questions, and he'd told them everything. Now they had that knowledge, he was no longer a person of interest, and it had left him feeling dirtied. He'd sold out in the hope of finding his clan, and instead he'd been cleaned out and left on the scrap heap. Yeah, he'd been used all right, and now what the fuck was he going to do? No one wanted to know him in here, just like no one had ever wanted to know him in the outside world either.

He finished his tray of food and carried it over to dump the scraps in the bin and stacked the empty tray on top of all the others. He had a little spare time before his work shift started. The idea of prisoners all sitting around in their cells all day was completely wrong. Nicholas had been given a job making clothing, which earnt him a pathetic amount for his commissary, so he could buy extra snacks or drinks, or even toiletries. They worked them hard for the pittance they were paid, but he guessed it wasn't as though he was in here to earn his fortune. The way things were going, he doubted he'd be in here long at all. At some point, someone would probably take a disliking to him and decide to end his life. There were plenty of people out in the real world who would say he got everything he deserved and would most likely raise a glass at the news of his death. The detective, Erica Swift, would be one of them, no doubt.

After lunch, the prisoner officers took the next shift, including Nicholas, back to the workshop. He kept his head down, focusing on each of the zips that needed to be attached to the jackets, ignoring everyone around him. Fish didn't work in here—he was on cleaning duty—so at least that was one person Nicholas didn't have to think about right now. He did worry, though—he fretted about later, when they were alone in their cell. Would Fish continue to act like a prick towards him, or would it all be forgotten and he'd be back to normal, asking Nicholas to tell the story about how he'd gouged the first man's eyes out?

Suddenly, something slammed into the backs of his knees, folding his legs in half. He hadn't had time to protect himself, and his chin hit the worktable as he went down. He smacked his chin. His teeth snapped together, and pain exploded through his tongue, his mouth filling with the iron tang of blood. He found himself on the floor, spitting blood and trying not to think too hard about why a large chunk of his tongue felt like it was missing.

"What the hell are you doing down there?" Officer Bache shouted from over by the door. "On your feet, and back to work."

Just like everyone else in this place, Officer Bache seemed to have taken an instant dislike to Nicholas. That he'd killed a police officer's husband hadn't done anything to enamour him to them. They saw that as though he'd murdered one of their own.

He wiped his mouth and put out a bloodied hand to pull himself back up to standing. He didn't even dare look around to see who had hit him. It didn't matter anyway, it wasn't as though he'd be able to retaliate. Everyone here had people who backed them up, while he was on his own.

The blood from his cut tongue continued to flow. He wasn't squeamish—at least not when it came to other people's blood—but the thick, hot fluid filled his mouth and threatened to spill down his throat. He ducked his head slightly to spit it on the floor. He couldn't get blood on the jackets, as he'd risk punishment.

He spat, the blood a vivid red against the concrete. How much blood was that? Too much. Still it came, flowing into his mouth, and he was forced to spit again.

"What the fuck, dude?" the prisoner next to him exclaimed, wrinkling his nose at the mess Nicholas had made.

He put his hand to his mouth. "Sorry." He shouldn't be sorry. He hadn't asked to be hit in the back of the legs and to bash his mouth so badly he'd bitten straight through his tongue, but he couldn't think of anything else he was supposed to say. Besides, his thoughts weren't working so clearly right now. He'd broken out in a cold sweat, his palms clammy. His legs hurt from where he'd been hit, but now they felt numb and as though they didn't really belong to him.

With a gut-wrenching certainty, he realised he was going to pass out, and he was going to do so in front of everyone. He couldn't have got any more pathetic if he tried.

Darkness swept into his vision, and for the second time in a matter of minutes, his legs gave way. He hit the floor hard but was unable to get his body to respond enough to protect his head. He was vaguely aware of voices shouting and people rushing over, before he passed out completely.

Chapter Eight

Erica dropped Poppy off at Breakfast Club at school and then drove into work. She was refreshed and clearheaded compared to the previous day. The sun was already warm, and it really felt as though summer had finally arrived. London had been lulled into a false sense of security when they'd had a couple of warm weeks over April, but then they'd been plunged back into grey skies and rain again up until now. Her mood was further improved by the knowledge Shawn was back in that morning, and the annoying sulking that DC Howard had been doing all week would come to an end. She intended on letting Rudd finish up the Skehan case, though there didn't appear to have been any developments on it overnight. Hopefully, something would come to light today that would allow them to move forward on it. Right now, they had nothing. It was as though Skehan's attacker had been plucked out of the back garden and had vanished.

Shawn was in the office when she arrived, his car already in his spot. He was clearly as keen to get back to work as she was to have him.

"Don't bother taking off your jacket," he said, walking towards her as she entered. "We're needed in Hackney. A call just came in. A woman's body's been discovered."

"No easing into things for you," she said. "Welcome back."

He grinned at her. "I expect the killer was just waiting for me to get to work."

"Good thing you're here then. Let's go."

THOUGH CRIME SCENE tape was stretched across the front door of the building, the flat where the woman had been killed was on the first floor. Erica pulled on a pair of gloves from her pocket and ducked under it, Shawn close behind. She trotted up the stairs and took the narrow hallway down to the flat. From the amount of activity around the open front door, it was easy to pinpoint the right one.

If there hadn't been the activity, they could have followed their noses. The air was ripe with the stench of death.

The police sergeant in charge of the scene was leaning over the bed as they entered. He was around Erica's age, mid-thirties, with a crop of curly russet hair and freckles across the bridge of his nose that made him look younger and less serious than he actually was.

He straightened. "Detectives, thanks for coming. I'm Sergeant Payne. Our victim is Naomi Conrad, twenty-seven years old, single, as far as we know. The body was found by the neighbours, Andrew and Melinda Long, after they noticed the smell."

The woman lying on the bed had long blonde hair and a slender figure. She was also naked. From the reek of death in the room, she had been dead for at least a couple of days.

"They'd ignored it at first," Sergeant Payne continued, "but eventually couldn't stand it anymore and so they knocked on the front door. When no one answered, Andrew Long tried the door handle and discovered it unlocked. He opened it and called out, but when they didn't get a response, they checked the rest of the flat, found the body, and called us."

"Any idea how long she's been dead?" Erica asked.

"At a guess, forty-eight hours, possibly a little longer, but it's hard to say for sure until the post-mortem. It's been warm these last couple of days, which is why the body was discovered. At first glance, it appears she's been strangled. I'm unsure yet if there was any sexual assault."

Erica frowned down at the body. What an absolute waste of a beautiful young woman's life. "Any witnesses?"

"Only the neighbours, so far, but I have officers going door to door. If we can nail down a more precise time of death, it'll make things easier when we're questioning the neighbours or checking on any CCTV."

The Scenes of Crime officer had already bagged the young woman's hands, in the hope the pathologist would be able to scrape DNA from beneath the nails. If she'd fought back while she was being strangled, she might have scratched her attacker.

Erica took in every detail—the empty wine glass, the discarded bundle of clothes, including the underwear, beside the bed. Though the victim's face was already showing some signs of bloating, it was easy to see she'd died wearing makeup, including false eyelashes. These girls always seemed to wear so much makeup these days, even when it was clear that, like Naomi Conrad, they were naturally beautiful.

"Looks to me like she'd come home from a night out," Erica observed. "Since the front door was unlocked, do we think her attacker came in that way?"

Payne nodded. "The windows around the flat were all locked from the inside, so it would appear that whoever killed her just walked out through the front door and down the communal hallway, down the stairs, and through the main front door."

Erica chewed on her lower lip. "I think we need to consider that Naomi Conrad knew her attacker."

"Most of them do," Payne agreed.

"What is it she did for a living?" Shawn asked.

"She's an"—Payne flicked inverted commas in the air with his fingers—"'influencer', apparently. Online stuff. Makeup and skincare and clothes."

Cardboard boxes were stacked in the corner of the bedroom next to a circular light on a stand.

"People were sending her stuff," Erica said. "So, they must have been able to get her address."

How careful were these people online? They put everything out there, shared every little intimate detail with hundreds of thousands of complete strangers. Had one of them contacted her, promising to send her a freebie that she could then advertise online, and they'd used her information to come to her flat and murdered her instead? It didn't matter how much they were warned about the dangers of being online, when they were young, they thought they were invincible.

"Does she live alone?" Erica asked.

"According to the neighbours, yes, she does. We can't find any sign of anyone else living here either.

"Any boyfriend on the scene?"

Payne twisted his lips. "We're not sure yet."

"What about family?"

He gestured to a shelf on the bedroom wall. "She has some photographs up, so we think she has parents, possibly a sister, too."

"We need to track them down. What about the rest of the flat? Was anything taken?"

"We haven't been able to find her mobile phone, so it's possible whoever did this took it with them."

"A memento, perhaps." Erica looked to Shawn. "Let's put a trace out on the phone. We might be in luck and whoever has taken it hasn't switched it off."

Naomi Conrad's phone would have had everything about her life on it. All her photographs, all her messages, her social media. Her contacts. If the assailant used her fingerprint to open it before killing her and then changed the code, he could have full access to it.

Sergeant Payne leaned over the body again and used a gloved hand to lift the victim's blonde hair from her neck, revealing the contusion marks. A flicker of recognition went through Erica, and she frowned. It was as though she'd just had a moment of déjà vu only even more real than normal. Like she'd just been propelled back in time, to a case from a year ago. It had been the lifting of the hair, where it had hidden the bruises and lacerations around the victim's neck that had done it. From the conjunctival petechial haemorrhage—the red dots on the whites of the eyes—it was clear the woman had been strangled, though until they had a final post-mortem report, it was impossible to know for sure. Strangulation was a common form of domestic abuse and may have been taken too far in this situation, but still, something about the setup rang bells in her head.

"What is it, boss?" Shawn asked from beside her.

She chewed her lower lip and looked around the room. "Does this remind you of anything?"

"Funny you say that, I was just thinking about that case with the brother and sister."

"Tristan Maher," she confirmed. "His sister was called Lara."

He nodded. "That's right."

Erica wasn't likely to forget their names any time soon. Tristan Maher had kidnapped her and was going to turn her into one of his paintings. It had happened right before her dad had died, and every detail of those events were burned into her brain. Tristan had been given several life sentences and would be lucky if he ever got to see freedom again, but she didn't know what had happened to Lara. She imagined the poor woman must have needed to have some serious therapy after living with that monster most of her life. How did it feel to know you shared so much DNA with a serial killer?

"What's that?" Payne asked.

"Just an old case we worked on," Erica said. "The victims were all women and strangled in their beds, but the perpetrator is serving several life sentences, so it can't be the same one."

"It's probably just a coincidence," Shawn said.

Erica raised her eyebrows. "I'm not sure I believe in coincidences."

Payne gestured to the victim. "Strangulation is a common method of murder. We're most likely looking at a man in her life who was trying to control her, someone she'd possibly already been experiencing violence at the hands of." He nodded at the lighting setup and the stack of boxes. "Perhaps someone didn't like the business she was in."

"A post-mortem will give us an idea of if there was any sexual activity before she died," Erica said. "We need to look into who Naomi Conrad was. Check if she has a record. I also want all the neighbours interviewed, find out if anyone saw her coming home a couple of nights ago, either alone or with someone. If we can get an idea when she came home, we can check any CCTV from around the area."

No one liked the idea of being caught on CCTV until they were the victim and wanted the police to catch whoever was the perpetrator of the crime.

Payne nodded. "I've got officers going door to door, see if anyone saw anything."

The similarities to the Tristan Maher case, the one the papers had called *The Artisan*, continued to niggle at her. Admittedly, the body hadn't been staged the same way as Maher had done with his victims—she hadn't been sitting up in bed, for example—but they'd never released details of how the victims had been arranged before he'd left them. They knew now that he'd done so in order to take photographs of the dead women, which he'd then used to recreate in oil on canvas. There had been so many cases, many of which overlapped, so she'd been dealing with more than one at a time, and it was hard to remember the exact details of everyone she'd dealt with.

"There was a time waster involved in that case, wasn't there?" Shawn said thoughtfully. "Do you remember? He pretended he'd been the one to kill those women."

She shot him a sharp look. "Yes, you're right. I don't suppose you remember his name?"

Shawn thought for a moment and shook his head. "Sorry, no, but it'll be in the case files."

"You think it's possible he's decided to take things a step further?"

"It's possible. We know it can't be Tristan Maher 'cause he's behind bars, and I'd say it's unlikely to be the sister. She would have been the same size as the victim and would have been evenly matched, unless she was drugged or something, which the post-mortem will reveal."

"You don't think this is just a coincidence then," she said. "You think this might be connected to the Maher case?"

"That's not what I'm saying, but you always say that we should keep our minds open to all possibilities when we're working on a case. This is just me, keeping my mind open."

It was true, she did say that.

She exhaled a breath and resisted the urge to rub her eyes—she was still wearing her gloves.

The Scenes of Crime officer emerged from the bathroom holding a clear bag with something inside it. "Thought you'd want to know about this."

Erica frowned at the item. A used condom. She grimaced. "I assume that's semen in the tip."

The officer lifted it to get a better view. "I'd say you're right."

She glanced over her shoulder at Shawn. "You think a killer would be stupid enough to have sex with his victim, strangle her, and then dispose of a used condom filled with his DNA into the bathroom bin?"

Shawn shrugged. "There are plenty of cases of criminals making stupid mistakes."

Erica considered all possibilities. "Or our victim was the one who put the condom in the bin, and the killer didn't notice."

He raised his eyebrows. "Or the condom doesn't belong to the killer."

That was probably more likely, but if that was the case, it wasn't going to help them at all. The DNA they'd get from the body and from the condom might belong to the wrong person.

"We're going to need to track down whoever that condom belonged to," Erica said. "Even if he wasn't the person who murdered Naomi Conrad, he might have seen or heard something that could help us."

She was determined to get more leads from the case than they currently had with the Skehan one. She refused to let another criminal go unpunished today.

Chapter Nine

Erica left the building and called DC Rudd. "Any updates on the Skehan case?"

It was normal for her to handle more than one case at a time. Not that Brandon's case wasn't important, but murders took precedence over assault, even if that assault was a vicious one with a knife.

She was going to need to ask Gibbs for some more detectives if their team was going to make progress on either of the cases.

"No big leads, I'm afraid. I'm worried this one is going to go cold on us."

"Me, too. What about the victim? How's he doing?"

"He's being discharged today, so he must be doing all right. He actually called the office and asked if he could speak to you. He said he'd remembered something about the attack."

A little jolt of hope went through her. Hopefully, he'd remembered something important. "Okay, I'll try and swing by before they let him out."

"I can do that, boss," Rudd offered.

"No, it's fine. He knows me now. It's better if I go."

She remembered her own self-talk about delegating. Perhaps this was one of those times where she should have let Rudd go, but she found she wanted to see Brandon Skehan herself.

Erica ended the call and turned her attention back to the new case.

Shawn stepped out onto the street, pulling off his gloves. The road had been closed at both ends, but the residents of the neighbouring properties were gawking out of windows or standing at their front doors, trying to get a better idea about what was going on.

"We need to inform the family," she told him. "They might be able to give us an idea who did this to her. We can find out if they knew if she was seeing anyone."

"The parents live in Enfield," Shawn said, checking.

"Good, not too far away."

It was a horrible task, but she always preferred to do it in person. It never felt right when the family lived a long distance from the victim and Erica had to send someone from a different force to break the news. Families could also provide vital information that could help them find the killer, and Erica didn't like to hear it secondhand. Of course, then there were the families who discovered, after a loved one's death, that they didn't know their child, or spouse, or parent at all, which made their loss even harder to bear. Perhaps, even worse, were those who didn't even care that something terrible had happened to their child. Often, the parents had divorced and hadn't spoken to their adult child in years. Somehow that made things even more unpleasant.

They drove to the address they had on record for Naomi Conrad's parents, Alan and Debbie Conrad.

A solid rock had formed in the middle of Erica's stomach at the knowledge she was about to blow these two poor people's worlds apart.

A young woman opened the door. The likeness to Naomi was startling—the same long blonde hair and wide hazel eyes. She blinked at Erica and Shawn. "Can I help you?"

Erica showed her ID. "Are you a relation to Naomi Conrad?"

"Yes, I'm her sister, Carina."

"Are your parents home?"

"Yes, they are. I don't live here, though, I've just popped round for a cup of tea. What's happened? Did something happen to Naomi?"

"It would be best if we could come in and speak to you all together."

An older woman's voice came from somewhere in the house. "Who is it, Carina?"

Carina called over her shoulder, "Two detectives. They want to talk to us about Naomi."

No response came back, but a moment later, Debbie Conrad appeared in the hallway behind her daughter. Erica could see where the two daughters had got their looks from. Debbie Conrad was in her sixties and was still a beautiful woman, despite the worry drawn across her features.

"Jesus, let them in then."

Carina moved out of the way, and Erica stepped through, Shawn close behind. Carina shut the front door behind them. They followed her into the adjacent room, where a man was sitting in front of the television, a game of golf on the screen.

"Turn that off, Alan. These are police officers."

He didn't say anything but picked up the remote control and hit a button to turn the screen black.

"What's happened to Naomi?" Debbie asked, the moment the television fell silent. "Is she all right? Is she hurt? She hasn't done something wrong, has she?"

Erica noted the question. Why would her mother ask that? Had Naomi got herself into trouble in the past?

"You should probably sit down, Mrs Conrad."

Her hand went to her chest. "Oh God, this is going to be bad, isn't it?"

Detectives tended not to make house calls when it was good news, unfortunately.

The older woman reached for her younger daughter's hand. Carina took it and perched on the armrest of the chair that her mother sank into.

"I'm sorry to inform you that Naomi's body was discovered this morning."

Carina's eyes grew wide. "What?"

Naomi's father, Alan, finally spoke up. "No, that can't be right. Are you sure it's her?"

Erica offered them a sympathetic smile. "We will need one of you to do a formal identification, when you're ready, but yes, we're sure it's her. I'm very sorry."

Debbie shook her head. "No, not Naomi. You're mistaken. She can't be dead. She can't be." Her voice broke, and she buried her face in her hands, a howl of anguish bursting from her lungs.

Her youngest daughter sat, stunned into silence.

"How...how did she die?" Alan Conrad asked, sitting forward in his chair.

Erica looked in his direction. "It would appear she was murdered, but our investigations are ongoing."

A gasp of shock and a cry of 'oh God' came from Naomi's mother and sister.

"I need to see her," Alan insisted.

"You can. There are certain procedures that need to be followed first, but then you can come down to the morgue and see her, and give a formal identification at the same time."

"When will that be?"

"I'm not sure yet, but it'll be soon."

"Who did it? Who hurt my daughter?" His tone was rigid, the tension and emotion he must have been holding inside him so impossible to keep in that he was practically vibrating with the effort.

"We're still working on that, Mr Conrad. If there's anything you can tell us that might help, we'd appreciate hearing it. When was the last time you heard from Naomi?"

"I'm not sure. A few days ago, I think."

Naomi's sister nodded in agreement. "Yes, same. A few days ago."

"You didn't think anything was wrong when you hadn't heard from her?" Erica checked.

"We often go a few days without speaking," Carina said. "Besides, she was still posting on social media."

"She was still posting?"

"Yes, I mean, it obviously wasn't live posts, but I didn't think about that at the time. She must have already had some scheduled before she died."

Erica shot a glance to Shawn. Was that how things had happened? Or had Naomi's killer posted them himself to make it seem as though Naomi was still alive? She'd have to get their digital forensics teams to try and figure it out, though without actually having Naomi's phone to hand, she didn't know how easily they'd be able to do that.

Erica changed topics. "Was Naomi in any kind of trouble that you're aware of?"

Alan shook his head. "No, not that we knew of."

"We understand that she made her money through social media. Did she mention to you that she was being trolled or anything like that?"

His face seemed to crumple, as though it had folded in on itself. "We didn't really understand all that. She told us she did promotional work for companies online."

Had Naomi's business been something she was ashamed of, so she didn't tell her parents exactly how it worked? Or was it just that they didn't really understand, and she couldn't be bothered to explain it?

"How long has she been doing the online work?" Erica asked.

"Only a couple of years. It's really taken off for her. She was always coming home with new clothes and beauty products, giving anything she didn't want to keep to her mother and sister." He threw a look over to where they sat.

Carina nodded and swiped tears from her face.

Erica gave them a sympathetic smile. "Was there anyone in her life who might have wanted to hurt her?"

He frowned. "Like who?"

"A boyfriend, perhaps?"

"She didn't have a boyfriend," Debbie cried. "She broke up with someone ages ago and she hasn't brought anyone else home since."

"What's the name of the ex she broke up with?" Erica gave Shawn a nod to jot it down. Perhaps it was a bad breakup and the ex had been harbouring a grudge.

"His name's David Quinn," Alan said, "but he was a decent bloke. I never got the impression he'd do anything to hurt her, and I think the breakup was amicable."

Erica glanced over at Carina. Tears streamed down her cheeks, but she wiped them away and nodded.

"It wouldn't be David. Dad's right. He wouldn't have hurt her. I think he lives somewhere up north now. I'm not even sure the two of them were still in touch."

"What about different men in her life? You were her sister. Maybe she told you things she might not have told other people." By other people, Erica meant their parents.

Carina's gaze darted between her mother and father, and Erica assumed she'd hit the nail on the head.

"Perhaps you could see us out?" Erica suggested.

"Yes, of course." She wiped away more tears and squeezed her mother's shoulder as she stood.

Grief seemed to have hollowed Debbie out. She was the shell of the woman she'd been only minutes before when she'd invited them into the house. Erica had to remind herself that they weren't the ones who'd done this to the family—it was whoever had killed Naomi, and they were the ones who'd find him.

"Someone will be in touch about formally identifying Naomi," Erica told Alan. She handed him a card. "But if you think of anything that might help us, please don't hesitate to get in touch."

He nodded and took the card, his face pinched with grief.

Erica and Shawn both left the room and headed down the hallway to the front door, Carina following them. They stepped outside, and Carina half closed the front door behind them. She was still crying, but that was to be expected. There would be many tears in the weeks, months, and even years to come.

"I couldn't say it in front of Mum and Dad," Carina said, "but Naomi met blokes all the time online, on dating apps and stuff. She didn't have any serious relationships, that I know of, and I'm sure she would have told me if she'd met someone."

She swallowed down a sob.

"Do you know which apps she used in particular?" Erica asked. "Her phone was missing from the flat, so we think whoever killed her may have taken it. Of course, there's always the chance she lost it while she was out, but we haven't been able to trace it yet."

Carina shrugged. "Just the usual ones."

"Is there any chance you'd know what your sister's password might be for those apps? If you tried to log on as her, could you figure it out?"

Her face paled. "You think whoever killed her might have been someone she met online?"

Erica nodded. "It's a line of enquiry we're keeping open, yes. Your sister was intimate with someone before she was murdered."

"Fucking bastard," she choked out.

Erica handed Carina her phone. "Do you think you could try?"

Carina sniffed and took the device. Erica had already unlocked it for her, and Carina navigated the phone with ease.

She typed on the tiny screen even faster than Erica could type on a full-sized keyboard.

"There's a few different combinations of passwords she might have used," Carina said as she brought up various websites. "I'll just have to keep trying them and hope I don't end up locked out."

"Do whatever you need to. Finding out who she met that night could be a huge leap towards finding her killer."

Erica stopped talking for a moment, allowing the other woman to concentrate.

Within less than a minute, Carina declared, "I'm in." She handed the phone back to Erica.

Erica studied the screen. Naomi had been sending lots of messages to different people, but there was one in particular that seemed to have a longer thread than the others. Erica opened it up and scrolled through. The profiles appeared to be under nicknames, rather than their full ones.

His final message was: *Hope you're still up for tonight? The Wilde Sage Wine Bar? 9pm?*

Her reply: *Can't wait.*

"Looks like she met up with someone on Tuesday evening."

The timing was a little earlier than she'd anticipated, but until they got the post-mortem report back, they'd just been guessing at her time of death. She could easily have been killed in the early hours of Tuesday morning rather than Wednesday evening.

Erica didn't know if the profile picture this person had used was correct, but at least they now had the name of the bar Naomi had gone to before she'd died. It was in Shoreditch. If they were in any luck, they'd be able to get CCTV from the bar and find out who she'd met.

Chapter Ten

Erica dropped Shawn back at the office, with instructions to hand what they knew over to digital forensics, and see if they could trace the person Naomi had been planning to meet, and then she headed back to the hospital. She hoped she wasn't too late to catch Brandon Skehan before he was discharged.

When she arrived, Brandon was sitting on the edge of the bed, back in regular clothes. He was on his phone but lifted his head as she walked in.

"You're looking better," she said with a smile.

He gestured down at his jeans and t-shirt. "No more ugly hospital gown. They said I could go home today, so I'm just waiting for them to officially discharge me. I've got a follow-up appointment as an outpatient and enough medication to start my own pharmacy, but I guess I'll survive."

"That's good to know. It could have been a lot worse."

He glanced down at his hands with his one good eye and nodded, no doubt picturing exactly how it could have been worse.

"To be honest," he said, cautiously, "I'm kinda nervous about going back to my flat. I'm a grown adult and all that, but the thought of being back there puts the shits up me."

"That's understandable. Don't you have a family member or a friend you could stay with?"

"All my family are back in Ireland, and I don't feel like I can put this on a mate. What if whoever did this decides to finish off the job and tracks me down to wherever I'm staying? I couldn't forgive myself if I got someone else hurt."

"The chances of that happening are extremely unlikely."

He pointed in her direction. "Ah, but not impossible, and there lies the problem, Detective."

"If it helps to ease your mind, we've had plenty of police presence on your street since all this has happened, and even though our forensics team have finished working on your place, I can get a squad car to drive past your flat every couple of hours, so if whoever did attack you is still hanging around, they'll know not to try anything."

"What about the times between the drive-by?"

"Brandon, I'm afraid it's impossible for us to watch out for you all the time." She didn't want to add that she was also dealing with a murder case right now and that her attention was diverted to finding a young woman's killer. Of course, no member of the public, and especially not a victim, wanted to hear that the police were too busy to give that one case all their attention. They were always having to juggle cases, and a murder trumped a case of grievous bodily harm. "The best way we can keep you safe is by catching who did this to you, and you can help us with that. When you called the office, you said you remembered something about the attack. What was that?"

"His shoes," he said. "I remembered what shoes the bloke who attacked me was wearing. They were trainers—white ones—and jeans, too."

Erica checked out Brandon's outfit. "Similar to what you're wearing now?"

"I guess so."

"What about the brand of trainers?"

He shook his head. "Sorry, I don't know what brand. It was dark."

"How about how tall your attacker was? For him to have cut you across the face, he must have got up pretty close. Were you able to even get a feel for his height or build? Did you see his hand around the knife, so you can give me an idea of skin colour?"

"He came up behind me, so it was hard to tell his height. I suppose he must have been my height or taller, though. It all happened so fast."

"Humour me for a moment," she said. She mimicked the action the attacker would have made, bringing the blade of an imaginary knife from left to right, starting at the inside of his nose on the right-hand side of his face and drawing it across, towards his right ear. "He brought the knife up, his arm wrapped around your head from behind. And cut you like this."

"That's right."

"So we know your attacker was right-handed," she said. "Then what happened?"

"I lashed out with my right arm and struck the attacker's, and the knife flew out of his grip and landed on the floor. I had blood all down my face, and my first instinct was just to run. I knew I couldn't fight when I couldn't see anything, and I thought he might have cut my eye out."

Erica frowned. "I wonder why your attacker didn't pick up the knife again before they took off. I would have expected them to, not only because they must have known they were leaving vital evidence behind, but also to use as a weapon should they be stopped again?"

He shrugged. "I started shouting for help the moment I ran. He must have got spooked and thought there wasn't time to pick it up again."

"Or he didn't want to get caught with a knife covered in blood," she mused.

His shoulders slumped. "I guess from all these questions that you're still no closer in finding out who attacked me?"

There was no point in lying to him. "Not yet, but I do have my best detectives working on the case."

"Guess I can't ask for much more than that."

A doctor—different to the one who'd told Erica off on the first night—entered the room.

"Looks like you're going to get that discharge," Erica told Brandon. "I'll leave you to it, but if there are any developments, I'll make sure you know about it."

"Thanks, Detective. Don't be a stranger." He gave her that lopsided smile again.

As Erica left the hospital room, she found herself smiling, too.

Chapter Eleven

Back in the office, Erica watched videos of Naomi Conrad online via her social media.

Even though Naomi had been English, she had a strangely American manner about her. The way she started her introduction with 'hey, guys' with the kind of enthusiasm Erica would expect from across the pond definitely had a US vibe. Naomi was bright and vibrant, but what kind of person lay beneath the whitened smile and the multiple layers of makeup? Who had wanted to kill her? Was a dark secret hidden behind that smile, or was she exactly the sort of person she displayed on her social media?

Erica had one of her constables going through each of Naomi's social media platforms in detail, running through the posts and comments, looking for anyone who might have been posting threatening comments, or simply something that didn't feel quite right. That didn't stop her scrolling through them herself, though, trying to get a better idea of who Naomi was and how she'd attracted a killer into her life. She also wanted to know if Naomi had scheduled her most recent posts, or if whoever had killed her had posted them for her, perhaps as a way to prevent people knowing she was already dead. But why would they want to hide that she was dead? To buy themselves more time? To do what?

Erica wasn't into social media—she simply didn't have the time to be on it—and frankly it terrified her to think that Poppy would be navigating all these sites in years to come. She knew as each year passed, the more the pressure would increase for Poppy to have her own phone and accounts. Her friends would all have them, and she'd be the odd one out. She'd start nagging Erica, and Erica knew she'd put her foot down and would be the bad guy. Trouble was, all the other kids in schools would have parents with nice, normal jobs. Jobs where they didn't have to stand over the body of a murdered twenty-something and try to figure out which sick bastard had killed her. Other parents could pretend the bad things they saw on the news wouldn't happen to people like them, but Erica knew differently. Bad things could happen to anyone at any time.

She kept scrolling, both fascinated and repelled by these clips into a stranger's life.

What could the killer have learned from the videos?

This time, as she watched Naomi's numerous clips, it was the background she sought out. What did the young woman's videos give away that she might not have noticed? The photograph of the family in the background. A piece of wall art that said 'single and lovin' it', a shot out of the window that gave a view onto the block of flats across the street. She'd thought it was possible the killer knew where Naomi lived because of her promotional work, but perhaps he'd simply caught sight of something in one of her videos that had given it away?

Shawn approached her desk. "I got hold of the manager at the wine bar Naomi Conrad arranged to meet her date at. He's free to speak to us."

"Great, let's go and have a chat."

They drove across the city and parked outside the wine bar. It was well into lunchtime, and the place was a busy bustle of young hipster and people in suits. As they entered, a woman in her early twenties approached with a smile.

"Do you have a reservation?"

"No, we're not here to eat. We need to speak to your manager, Thomas Croft." Erica showed the woman her ID.

"Oh, right. I'll just go and check if he's free."

"He's expecting us," Shawn said.

She flashed him another smile and then hurried to the back of the wine bar where she vanished through a door. A moment later, she returned with a man in his early thirties, casually dressed in a white shirt with the sleeves rolled up and a pair of jeans.

"Detectives," he greeted them. "I'm Thomas Croft, the manager. Do you want to come through to my office? It'll be a bit quieter in there."

Between the chatter of all the customers and the music playing in the background, it was hard to hear much. They followed him back through the door the hostess had gone through. The din from the bar decreased the moment the door swung shut behind them.

Thomas led them into his office and gestured for them to take a seat opposite his desk. The room was filled with boxes of promotional materials, coasters and pens sticking from the tops, reminding Erica of Naomi Conrad's bedroom. Had she done any promotional work for the bar?

"What can I do for you both?" the manager asked.

Erica pulled up a photograph of Naomi that she'd downloaded from her social media. "Do you recognise this woman?"

He studied the photo and frowned. "No, I'm sorry, I don't. Should I?"

"She came to the bar on Tuesday night. We believe she met a man here. Not long after she left, she was murdered in her bed."

"Jesus, that's awful. What can I do to help?"

"We need to track down the man she met. They arranged to meet here at nine p.m., and we'd like to see any CCTV footage you might have around that time."

"That's easy enough to do. I can show you now, if you like?"

Erica offered him a smile. It was so much simpler when people were cooperative. "That would be very helpful, thanks."

"Just give me a minute.

He turned to his computer and brought it to life. Erica and Shawn waited patiently while he located the CCTV files and scrolled back to the right time and date. He angled the screen so they could see it as well.

Erica watched, searching the throng of people at the bar for Naomi. Plenty of customers were standing, or sitting on stools, but none of them were her. Erica checked the time on the footage. It was ten past nine now; Naomi was late. Erica switched from watching for Naomi to trying to figure out if any of the men were the one Naomi was meeting. They all had a similar style about them, as though they'd all been dressed by the same designer.

A blonde woman approached the bar, and one of the men turned to greet her, standing from the stool. He leaned in and kissed her cheek.

"That's her," Erica said. "I'm sure of it."

"Do you want me to pause the video?" the bar manager asked.

"No, keep it running until we can see both their faces clearly."

It only took another few seconds for that to happen. As the couple lined up, side by side at the bar, the camera was able to get a good shot.

"Yes, that's Naomi," Erica confirmed. "Now to figure out who she's with."

The man appeared to be in his late twenties to early thirties. He was attractive, with tattoos running down his arms in sleeves, and a tight shirt that showed off the kinds of muscles that could only be got after some serious gym sessions. He ordered some drinks and then paid with a card.

Erica pointed at the screen. "There. That's what we can use to find him. I assume you have a record of your card payments."

"Of course. I've still got the receipts."

"Great." She turned to Shawn. "We're going to have to push this as being urgent. We can't afford to be waiting for days to get a name."

He nodded. "Agreed."

She looked back to Thomas. "We'll also need to interview the bartender who served the couple."

"His name is Lee Cerny. He's not in until later."

"Not a problem. If you give me his address, I'll send one of my detectives to his home to ask him some questions."

They were one step closer to finding out who Naomi Conrad had been with that night and if he was the one who'd killed her.

• • • •

A COUPLE OF HOURS LATER, the subpoena came through for the name and address of the man who used the credit card. The bank informed them that the credit card belonged to a Mr Robert Day and gave them his address.

Robert Day lived in a gated complex of newbuild flats on the Isle of Dogs. Erica pulled the car up to a microphone pillar in front of a huge metal gate and wound down the window. She reached out and pressed a buzzer to get the attention of security.

"I'm with the police. We'd like to have a word."

The gate slid back, and they drove into a car park filled with BMWs, Audis, and Mercedes. Around the car park were a semi-circle of buildings. It was about six stories, and while the newbuild flats weren't massive, they still would have cost a pretty penny to either rent or buy.

The concierge—a young Asian man in a badly fitting suit—left the office to meet them.

They climbed out of the car and slammed the doors shut behind them.

Erica showed her ID. "We'd like to speak to Mr Robert Day, is he in?"

"I don't keep track of who's in or not," he said. "I'm more here to deal with people who lose their keys or take in packages or call in someone if there's a problem with the swimming pool."

"That's fine," she said. "We can go and knock to see if he's home." She jerked her chin at the security cameras either side of the door. "Are those things all over the complex?"

He nodded. "Pretty much. They're definitely in all the main entrances."

"So they'd catch it if someone came home or left again?"

He shrugged. "Unless that person went out of their way not to be seen, I suppose so."

Erica exchanged a glance with Shawn. It might help them pin down Robert Day's version of events on the night Naomi was murdered.

"Mr Day is in number three-oh-six. It's that way," the concierge said. "Third floor. You can take the lift."

"Thanks. We may be back to ask you some more questions and request some CCTV footage from a couple of nights ago."

"No problem. Whatever I can do to help."

Erica and Shawn set off in the direction the concierge had pointed. They pushed through doors into the entrance lobby of one of the buildings.

Shawn let out a low whistle and nodded to a sign about the private swimming pool, gym, and sauna. "Mr Day does pretty well for himself, then."

They caught the lift up to the third floor and then exited into a corridor. The place had a feel more of a hotel than a block of flats. They found the number they needed, and Erica rang the bell.

The man they'd seen on the CCTV footage at the wine bar answered the door. "Yes?"

"Mr Day? Robert Day?"

"Robbie," he said. "I go by Robbie."

"My name is DI Swift, and this is my colleague, DS Turner. Do you know a Naomi Conrad?"

"Naomi? Yeah, I do. Why? What's going on?"

"We'd like to come in and speak to you, if that's all right."

"I suppose so." He moved out of the way.

Erica and Shawn walked through. The flat was small, but it was brand-new. Erica peeped through each door as they passed—a bathroom, a double bedroom, a separate kitchen, and a living room that had a set of double doors leading onto a Juliette balcony with a view over the car park. Robert gestured for them to sit on the leather sofa, and he perched in the single armchair beside the balcony doors.

"Nice place you've got here," said Shawn.

"Thanks. It's all right."

Shawn looked around the room. "What do you do for a living?"

"I work in media—film editing, to be precise."

Shawn jutted his lower lip and nodded approvingly. "Must pay well."

Even though this wasn't huge, places in this part of London went for a fair penny.

"I do all right." Robert Day turned to Erica. "What's all this about? Is Naomi all right? She hasn't replied to any of my messages."

Erica kept her expression neutral. "How do you know Naomi?"

"We met online."

She tweaked her lips in a smile. "Humour me, Mr Day. I'm not as young as you and everyone I've met has been in person. How exactly do you go about meeting someone online?"

He gestured with his hand. "Well, we first met on a dating app, but then we started following each other online. Through social media."

"But then you met up in person?" she prompted. "When was the first time?"

"A few weeks ago."

"And how often have you seen each other since?"

"It wasn't a regular thing or anything. We met in person a few times, maybe five or six."

Shawn scribbled some notes down in a pad. Erica waited until he was done and then resumed the questions.

"When was the last time you saw Naomi in person?"

His hand went to his mouth, pinching his lips, and his gaze darted between the two detectives. "A couple of nights ago. We hooked up, you know. A few drinks, and then back to her place."

"How was the relationship between the two of you then?"

"It was good. Fine." His teeth dug into his lower lip. "Look, are you going to tell me what's happened? Clearly there is something very wrong? Did Naomi make a complaint against me or something?"

"Why would you think that? Was there violence between the two of you?"

He raised his voice. "No! Never. We were good. I'm just trying to figure out why I have two detectives sitting in my flat, questioning me about Naomi."

"So the two of you didn't argue?"

Twin spots of red appeared in his cheeks. "No. I already told you. We were fine. Please, just tell me what's happened."

"I'm afraid Naomi's body was discovered this morning."

His jaw dropped. "What?"

"She was killed in her flat a couple of days ago."

"Killed? Do you mean murdered?"

"Yes, I do," Erica said. "And we believe you might have been the last person to see Naomi Conrad alive."

"We think she was murdered the same night you met up with her, though we'll know a more precise time of death once the post-mortem has been conducted."

"Oh, shit." His face drained of colour. "You don't think I have something to do with it?"

Erica studied his reaction for any sign of guilt or that he was hiding something. "We don't know, Robbie. That's why we're here, so we can find that out. We need to ask you some questions. We'd like you to come down to the station so we can conduct a formal interview."

"I'll do whatever it takes to help. Naomi was a sweet girl. I mean, I didn't know her all that well, but she wasn't all glamorous and overconfident like she is online. She's actually pretty shy."

"We can drive you down now, if you like?" Erica said. It sounded like an offer, but she didn't intend to let him say no.

But she need not have worried.

Robbie got to his feet. "Let me grab my stuff."

· · · ·

AN HOUR LATER, THE three of them sat in one of the interview rooms down at the station. They'd offered him a solicitor, but he'd declined. For the sake of the recording, she'd read Robert Day his rights, and run over the same questions she'd asked at his flat.

"You said you met up with Naomi just after nine. Can you tell me about the hours preceding that? How did your day start?"

He shrugged. "Just like any other. I got up and went to work. I needed to finish a job, so I stayed late and got back about seven. That gave me enough time to have something to eat and grab a quick shower and then I left to meet Naomi at the Wilde Sage Wine Bar in Shoreditch."

"How did you get to the bar?"

"I caught the Tube and walked the rest of the way."

"Did anything unusual happen that day? Did you notice anyone suspicious hanging around?"

Robbie looked between them. "No, I didn't."

"What about phone calls between you and Naomi? Did you speak to her that day?"

"We sent a couple of messages back and forth confirming tonight and saying we were looking forward to seeing each other, but that was all."

"And are you seeing anyone else you've met online? Or even people you know in real life?"

Robert Day was young, attractive, and wealthy. She doubted he and Naomi were exclusive after only a few weeks.

"I'm in touch with other girls I've had hook-ups with, if that's what you mean, but I'm not currently sleeping with anyone else."

"What about Naomi? Do you know if she was seeing anyone else?"

He gave a small, nervous laugh. "That's not really something we talked about."

She offered him a smile of reassurance and jotted down some notes. "Did she ever mention feeling unsafe, or that someone was out to hurt her?"

He shook his head. "No, never. She dealt with plenty of trolls online, but that's just part of the job. Everyone in her business deals with that kind of thing."

"So there wasn't anyone in particular that she mentioned to you?"

"No. I wish there was, so I could point you in the right direction, but those trolls hide behind fake profiles." He swiped at his eyes and shook his head. "God, I can't believe she's dead. She was so alive, so full of energy and excitement for what she was going to achieve in her life. She would have done it, too, everything that she'd dreamed of. That was just who she was."

Shawn clasped his hands on the table. "You seem to know a lot about her considering you've only really known her a few weeks."

He shrugged, but colour bloomed in his cheeks. "I'd been following her on social media, too."

Shawn frowned. "Doesn't she post about makeup and skin care and things like that?"

His colour deepened. "She's a gorgeous girl. I enjoyed watching her." He must have realised what he'd said as he blinked rapidly. "That sounds bad. I don't mean stalking her or anything. Just following her social media profiles, like everyone does."

Erica took back over. "What happened on Tuesday evening after you'd met up?"

He blinked back at Erica. "Nothing unusual. We had a couple of drinks there and then went back to her place 'cause it's closer."

"Where she was later murdered."

He put up both hands. "Hey, she was completely alive when I left her, I swear it. She was fine. More than fine. We'd both had a great night."

Shawn pursed his lips. "You didn't want to stay the night with her, though?"

"There's nothing against leaving after a hook-up. That's all it was. We weren't in a relationship or anything. She seemed happy enough for me to leave. We said we'd do it again sometime."

"Did she mention being worried about anything or anyone?" Erica asked. "Did you notice anyone unusual hanging around?"

"Wait a minute." He sat up straighter. "I *did* see someone. Another bloke. He pushed in the front door when I was on my way out."

Erica frowned. "The front door, as in Naomi's, or the main one for the building?"

"The main one for the building. I didn't question it or anything. I mean, I didn't live there, so I don't know who should or shouldn't be coming in. He just kind of gave me a nod and kept going."

"And what time was this?"

"Late. Must have been about one-thirty. I don't remember checking the time exactly, but we got back to the flat just before midnight, so yeah, I guess it would have been about half one."

Shawn leaned forward. "Can you give us a description of this man?"

"About my age, I guess. Brown hair. My sort of height. I think he was wearing jeans, but I didn't really pay that much attention, plus I'd had a few drinks that night, so my memory is a bit hazy."

Erica raised her eyebrows and struggled to keep the sarcasm from her tone. "That's convenient. You're saying that you just happened to see someone who looks a bit like you going into the same building where the woman you'd just been with was murdered."

He widened his eyes. "I'm telling the truth. It's not my fault that's the way it happened."

Erica kept her voice level. "Do you understand how this appears, Mr Day? Your DNA is most likely going to be all over the body. Other than her killer, you were the last one to see her alive. And now you're telling us some other man happened to enter the building at the same time you left."

"I'm not lying!" Fear brightened his eyes. It was clear the repercussions of that night had dawned on him. "Hang on, don't you need some kind of motive? I didn't have any reason to kill her. I barely knew her."

She arched an eyebrow. "Maybe the strangling was a sexual kink that went too far?"

"What? No, I'm not into things like that."

Shawn threw in a suggestion. "Or something went wrong during sex and she laughed at you or embarrassed you, and you got angry."

Tears shimmered in his eyes. "You're just making stuff up now. Nothing like that happened. We had a good time and I left, that's all."

"Did you take her phone with you?"

"Why would I have done that?"

"Because it was missing from her flat when we found the body. Unless she lost it during her night out, we think whoever killed her took it."

He shook his head. "She didn't lose it. She had it in the flat when I left. She was checking her social media while we were lying in bed. She's into all that kind of thing—I mean, she was. She was showing me some of her photos and some of her recent videos she'd already recorded that she was planning to post. She got paid money to do all that. Good money."

"And she definitely had the phone when you left."

Robbie looked between them as though he thought eye contact alone could save him. "Definitely. I swear."

"Would you be willing to give a DNA sample and fingerprints so we can rule you out of the investigation?" Erica asked him.

"I think I should get that solicitor before I do or say anything else."

"By all means, it's within your right to do so." Erica preferred it when they had a solicitor with them. It meant that if things came down to a conviction, any evidence gathered during the interview was less likely to be thrown out of court.

His nostrils flared, and he nodded, glancing down at his hands. "I will. Not that I did anything to her, but I don't want you to make out like I did."

"Our job is to find the person who did this, not simply arrest someone who happened to be in the wrong place at the wrong time. We want fingerprints and a DNA sample to rule you out of the investigation, not convict you wrongly." She caught his eye. "We want to find whoever did this to Naomi, too."

Chapter Twelve
Eighteen Months Earlier

Life behind bars was a daily grind for Nicholas. He did his best to keep his head down, but he seemed to draw attention from all the wrong people.

His tongue had been sutured with dissolvable stitches after the incident in the workshop, but the chunk he'd taken out of it when he'd bitten it had left him with a slight lisp that only gave the other inmates another reason to pick on him. They never did it where one of the prison officers could see, and it was always subtle, or just enough to make it seem as though he'd fallen or tripped. One of the prison officers themselves wasn't much better. Officer Bache had also taken a dislike to Nicholas, and while he didn't take part in the physical violence himself, he was more than happy to turn a blind eye if he walked in on something.

Nicholas doubted there were many out there who'd feel sorry for him, but that didn't stop him feeling sorry for himself.

A clang of keys on metal drew his attention, and he looked up from his book to see Officer Bache outside his cell.

"Mail for you, Bailey."

Nicholas sat up straight. He never got any letters. No one in the outside world gave a shit enough about him to want to put actual pen to paper. He was alone in this world, Erica Swift had seen to that when she'd let his brother, Danny, die.

His heart did a strange trip. Would it be her? Would she have written to him? She might have penned a letter filled with hatred towards him because of what he'd done to her husband, or perhaps she'd found God and decided to forgive him and felt the need to let him know that.

Bache waved the letter between the bars. "You going to take it or not? I'm more than happy to use it as toilet paper to wipe my arse on later if you don't want it."

Nicholas jumped down and took the letter, and then went back to his bunk. Fish glanced over with bored disinterest, not caring about Nicholas's post.

Nicholas lay on his back and held the letter up to study the front of the envelope. It had already been opened, of course, the contents studied by prison staff and approved before being handed over to him. They'd want to make sure it wasn't anyone planning something like an escape or trying to smuggle in drugs.

He didn't recognise the scrawled handwriting on the envelope—not that he'd expected to—but still he studied each line and curve. He wanted to savour the moment of actually having something interesting and different in his life. Prison was, if nothing else, monotonous. He woke at the same time every day, ate at the same time, working the same number of hours. Each day he was allowed one hour of fresh air. Nothing ever changed, except for the variation in whatever ways his fellow inmates decided to torture him.

This letter, though, that was different. He brought it to his nose and inhaled, imagining he could scent the aftershave or even perfume of whoever had written it. He couldn't, of course, it just smelled of paper and ink, and a little of the musty odour of the prison, but he enjoyed the sensation. He turned it over in his hands, inspecting the back for anything that might give him a clue as to who it was from, but there was nothing. The postage stamp didn't give anything away either, and the prison staff had stamped a large 'approved' over the top of it.

With care, he opened the envelope and drew out the letter inside and unfolded it. It was handwritten in blue pen. There was no address in the top right-hand corner, and no date either.

Dear Mr Bailey,

You don't know me, but it seems we share a number of common interests, and I was hoping to strike up an old-fashioned pen pal friendship where we might discuss our shared hobbies. I have many things I like to do outside of work. Sometimes I find city living to be stifling and I take myself out into the countryside, to walk and breathe the fresh air. I'm a fan of nature and wildlife in general. I've been a keen birdwatcher in my time, and that's definitely something I hope to take up more of in the months to come.

I hope to hear from you soon,

M Cimi.

Nicholas stared down at the letter. What was he supposed to make of it? He'd never had any interest in wildlife. Living in inner city London his whole life meant he'd rarely seen anything more than a pigeon pecking around on the pavement, or a rat scurrying down a Tube line, or very occasionally, an urban fox scavenging around dustbins late at night. And he was certain he didn't know a M Cimi. What did the 'M' stand for? Michael? Max? Martin? Was it even a man? The letter writer could be a woman. The tone felt male, though he didn't know why. He racked his brains trying to think of someone he knew with that name, but he drew a blank. He read the letter over once more, making sure he hadn't missed something. Was it possible that this M Cimi had the wrong prisoner? Perhaps he'd got Nicholas mixed up with someone else and had written the wrong name on the envelope? He had no fucking clue who that person might be, but he couldn't think of any explanation.

There wasn't even an address anywhere on the letter, so he didn't understand how this M Cimi thought he could write back. Was he supposed to already know the address? That thought only solidified the idea that the letter had been written to the wrong person.

Had any of the other prisoners here ever expressed an interest in wildlife? It wasn't the sort of conversation he'd start—not that he'd be inclined to start any conversation really. Those early days where his fellow inmates had been excited to hear what he had to say were long gone, and now they either rolled their eyes or just turned their backs on him if it looked as though he was trying to engage them in any way.

Even if he had an address to write back to, he wasn't sure he had anything to say. He'd never been much of a writer and hadn't exactly paid attention at school. He'd thought the whole thing was a total waste of time, and besides, he'd been more focused on the total shitshow of his home life than he had worried about school. After his mum had died and his brother had buried her in the back garden, he'd pretty much fallen apart. Schoolwork had been the last thing on his mind.

What would he say, even if he was able to find out an address? Would he tell Cimi that he most likely had the wrong person? That would probably be the best thing to do, but Nicholas had enjoyed receiving the letter. If he told him, then Cimi wouldn't write again, and Nicholas would once more have nothing to look forward to. Besides, he was lonely in here.

He could use a friend, even if it was one who thought he was someone else and who wanted to discuss something Nicholas had no interest in.

. . . .

WEEKS TURNED INTO MONTHS, and Nicholas had all but forgotten about the strange letter he'd received. He chalked it down to a case of mistaken identity. He hadn't heard if there was another prisoner here with the surname of Bailey, but it was a possibility. There were, after all, almost a thousand prisoners here, and it wasn't as though his name was unusual. Maybe it had been sent to the wrong prison, and that was what explained the mix-up.

Nicholas discovered that he didn't really care. He had more important things to worry about, like trying not to get beaten up in the showers, or have his meals knocked onto the floor at every mealtime, so he was forced to live on whatever he could buy at the commissary. He'd never been a particularly bulky man, but now his ribs jutted beneath his skin like a bird cage.

He lay in bed reading. It was one escape that he appreciated now he was in here. In the outside world, he wouldn't have dreamed of picking up a book, but things were different inside. He enjoyed his visits to the library, scanning the shelves for his next read and swapping the pile of books for a new set. There was a small television in their cell, but Fish got to decide what to watch on that, and Nicholas didn't dare argue with him. He could have saved up enough money to buy a radio from the commissary, but that would have meant playing it over the top of Fish watching television, and he was never going to do that.

When he was reading, he was silent, and silent people were easier to forget about.

One of the officers stopped outside the cell and pushed a letter onto the metal tray. "Post for you, Bailey."

Nicholas sat up, his heart beating faster. Instantly, his thoughts went to the mysterious letter-writer from months before. It might not be the same person, of course, but no one else had written to him.

He hopped down from the bunk, snatched the letter, and climbed back up again. The handwriting on the front was the same, and he pulled the envelope open and unfolded the letter inside.

Dear Mr Bailey,

I don't know if you're like me, but I was never particularly academic at school. That's not to say I wasn't clever—I like to believe I'm smarter than the everyday man—but I found the routine of school classes to be a drudge. Education isn't something that can be taught in the classroom, but instead should come from living. Don't you agree? Those who truly experience life by throwing themselves into it with all their being, but not allowing rules and expectations and others' opinions to get in the way are the ones who learn the most. Books are wonderful inventions, and I'd never be without them, but nothing beats getting your hands dirty. Recently, I've discovered a love of art. To walk through the respectful silence of a gallery is one thing, but to create that art yourself is something else. Not that I believe my talents to be any good, really—or perhaps they are and I'm being hard on myself—but there is something about the scent of oil paints and solvent in the air that makes me feel alive. It means something to create, to take a blank canvas and transform it into a piece of art that has meaning. I even enjoy scrubbing the paint from my hands afterwards, the way the red paint swirls against the white porcelain of the sink.

Nicholas stopped reading and lifted his head, his heart beating faster. The description of the paint against porcelain reminded him of blood. Had that been Cimi's intention? Cimi must have known what Nicholas had done—it wasn't difficult to find out. Unless Cimi had got the wrong prisoner number and was writing to the wrong inmate. But then why was he addressing him by name if he thought he was writing to someone else?

Nicholas bent his head again and continued.

Is art something you like to do, Nicholas? Do you like to create? I think as human beings, it's natural for us to create something, even if it's not in the traditional sense. But then, maybe some of us are more prone towards destruction?

Your friend,

M Cimi

Nicholas had never been into art. He'd done the subject at school and had liked it more than maths or science, but that hadn't been because of any particular love for the subject. His enjoyment had come more from the fact he saw it as the easy option. He wasn't too bad at it either—could draw a bowl of fruit or sketch a landscape and someone else would have been able to tell what it was. He'd never have claimed to have any particular talent or love for the subject, however, and he couldn't remember the last time he'd bothered to draw something. He liked receiving these letters from the mysterious M Cimi, though, and he didn't want to give the other man a reason to stop writing to him.

He checked the letter for any sign of a return address he could write to, but there was nothing. Who was Cimi, and why didn't he give Nicholas a way of writing back to him?

With a sigh, Nicholas sank back into the thin mattress, the letter still held in his hand. He hoped the next letter would bring more information, should there be a next one.

Chapter Thirteen

While they waited for Robert Day's solicitor, Erica put in a call to SOCO to get his flat searched for evidence. If he was guilty, she hoped they'd find the missing phone, but she had a feeling they weren't going to find anything. Robert Day had been more than happy to give his permission for them to search the flat, so they didn't need to get a warrant. Either he was extremely confident he hadn't brought any evidence from Naomi's murder with him back to the flat, or he was innocent.

"What do you make of Robbie Day, then?" Erica asked Shawn as they made their way to the coffee machine for a refill.

Shawn punched numbers on the machine. "I'm not sure. He seems genuine enough, and he's clearly a smart guy. Assuming the semen in the condom matches his, I'd say he'd have to be damned stupid to murder a woman and then leave a balloon chock full of his DNA in the bin."

"And he doesn't seem like a stupid man," she said.

"No, he doesn't. To do what he does for a living must take some brain power."

"He might have murdered Naomi in a moment of passion," she suggested. "Perhaps they were into choking during sex, and he panicked and fled the scene. He might not have thought about the DNA until later."

The first of the coffees dropped into the bottom of the machine, and Shawn fished it out. "Or he thought there was no point in trying to hide that he'd been with her, since there were already messages between them saying when and where they were meeting, plus CCTV of them together at the bar. He wouldn't have been able to deny that they were together."

Erica took the coffee from him. "But he might have been able to deny being at her flat?"

Shawn turned back to the machine to repeat the process for his own drink. "We already agreed he must be smart to have achieved what he has at his age. He must have known his DNA would be all over that flat."

"Then there's the mysterious man he saw. It's pretty lucky for him that he just happened to see someone entering the building as he was leaving. And that the person just happened to look a bit like he did."

Shawn took his drink from the machine. "So, if anyone else saw him and described him, he'd be able to say it was the other bloke."

"Exactly." Erica shifted the cup into her other hand, the hot liquid burning through the plastic.

Shawn turned to face her. "And that stuff about the phone? He said that she'd been showing him pictures and videos that she'd already had recorded that she'd been planning on posting. As we know, she continued to post even after she was dead, which means she'd either already set it up to post automatically, or else the killer posted those videos. If he was the one to post, might he also have commented on one of those posts?"

"If the killer was the one to set up those posts, we have to ask ourselves why? Why go to the trouble of making it appear as though Naomi was still alive?"

"He was buying himself time?" Shawn suggested.

"Time to do what?"

"Make an escape?"

Erica let out a long sigh. "Let's hope not. And there's still the possibility that we're looking in completely the wrong place. I haven't been able to shake the feeling that I've worked on a case like this before."

He arched an eyebrow. "Are you talking about the Maher case again?"

She dragged her hand through her hair. "I don't know. Something about it is bugging me. It was the way the hair was draped around the victim's throat to hide the strangulation marks. We released that information to the public, didn't we? It was the part about how he used to stage them that we kept quiet."

Shawn shook his head. "Honestly, I can't remember, and we had a leak as well, with that other man who came forward. I remember he was a weird one. He was obsessed with your cases and had newspaper clippings pasted all over his walls. But it's hard to recall all the details without going back over the files."

"Can you check them for me? Find out the name of the man who came forward and claimed to be the killer in the Maher case."

"Yeah, no problem."

They couldn't move any further forward with Robert Day until after his solicitor had arrived, and that could take hours. She might as well put her time to good use and put that nagging voice in her head to rest.

Chapter Fourteen

Erica was surprised Lara Maher hadn't moved out of London. Not only that, she hadn't even moved out of the house she'd shared with her psychopath brother, the same place he'd brought Erica himself when he'd kidnapped her.

Standing on the front doorstep now, every muscle in her body tensed. Though she knew Tristan Maher was safely behind bars, and that Lara hadn't played any deliberate part in his crime, with the exception of not calling them the moment she'd found the paintings and photographs, there was no reason to feel so anxious. This was just a simple building of brick and slate, no different to her own home. The person who'd lived there hadn't somehow infected the place.

She could have asked Shawn to come with her, but she felt better if she spoke to Lara alone. Lara had suffered abuse at her brother's hand for years, and Erica had no way of knowing what kind of emotional or psychological state she would be in. She might not react too well to having a man in the house again—even if that man was a detective—and would be more likely to open up to Erica.

Erica lifted her hand to the doorbell, clenched and unclenched her fist, and then pressed the buzzer. Somewhere in the house, a bell jingled.

She sucked in a breath and took a couple of paces back. Was there any movement inside the property? There was always the chance Lara might not be home. She'd run her own business when her brother had been apprehended for murdering those poor women, but Erica had no idea if she still did. Would people really allow Lara into their homes to clean after learning what her brother had done? It was hard to imagine feeling comfortable with that, even though it hadn't been Lara's fault. But that kind of thing had a way of tainting people.

Light footsteps approached from inside, and the door swung open a crack. It was halted by a security chain, and a chunk of face peered through the gap.

"Lara?" Erica said. "I don't know if you remember me—"

She didn't get any further. The door shut again, and for a moment Erica didn't think it would reopen, but then it did, and fully this time.

"Of course I remember you, DI Swift," Lara said. "How could I possibly forget?"

"I wondered if I'd be able to come in for a chat. It's nothing official. Just something that's been bugging me."

She let Erica in. "Yes, come in. I'll make some tea."

Erica hadn't exactly planned for this to be a social call either, but she didn't have the heart to refuse. She couldn't imagine what Lara's life must have been like after everything that had happened.

"Go through." Lara nodded towards the living room.

She vanished into the kitchen to make the tea, and Erica found herself unusually anxious as she took a seat, deliberately positioning herself so she had her back to the conservatory that Tristan had used as a painting studio. It was the same place she'd woken bound after he'd kidnapped her.

Lara came in with two mugs of tea in one hand and a bowl of sugar in the other. She set them down on the coffee table.

"I didn't know how you took it."

"No sugar is fine, thanks." She wasn't about to start telling Lara she was more of a coffee drinker and she liked it black and strong. When you were British, everyone assumed you drank tea.

Lara sat and clasped her hands together. "I'm guessing you're here about that poor woman who was murdered."

It had been all over the news. Lara was bound to have made a mental connection between the murder and what her brother had done.

"Yes, I am. I wanted to ask you a couple of questions, if that's all right."

She shrugged one shoulder. "Go for it, though I'm not sure what I can tell you."

"Are you still in touch with Tristan?"

Lara nodded and stared at her hands. "We write. I went in to visit him one time, not long after he was put inside. I don't know what I was expecting. Maybe I thought he'd change and that he would have realised just how much pain he'd caused and apologise, but he did nothing of the sort. He never thought he did anything wrong. It was as though the world owed him everything, and so he just took whatever he wanted."

"But you write? What sort of things does he say?"

"I write to him, but I don't read his replies. I tear them up and put them in the bin the moment they arrive."

"Why?"

"Because I don't want to read whatever it is he has to say. I know none of it will be good. I write to him because, despite everything, I don't want him to think that I've completely abandoned him. Maybe I should, but I shared a womb with him. I can't just pretend that he's dead."

Erica offered her a small smile. "No one is expecting you to do that. You have to do whatever it is that works for you as an individual. Nobody in the world has ever gone through what you have before, so it's impossible for anyone to tell you how or what you should be thinking or feeling."

Lara bit at her lower lip, working off a piece of dried skin. "You probably think it's weird that I've stayed in the same house, too, don't you?"

"I'm not going to judge your choices, Lara." In truth, she had thought it was odd, and clearly even Lara had realised that by her question.

Her voice dropped a level. "It's my home. It always has been. My parents left this place to me, and it's the only connection I have left to them, except for my car. With Tristan in prison and them dead, it felt like by selling it, I was purposefully trying to cut them out of my life. To forget them all and move on." She blew out a breath, and her eyes slid shut for a moment. "I couldn't bring myself to do that."

Sadness radiated from the other woman. Erica couldn't imagine how it must feel to learn something like that about the person you loved most in the world. How did you piece that together in your heart to ever sit right?

Lara looked up with a fake, bright smile. "Anyway, you're not here to ask me about how I'm doing, are you? I'm not naïve enough to think the police do that. You want to ask me about the case."

"You're right. The young woman was strangled in her home and left on the bed, naked."

Lara jumped straight to the point. "You mean like Tristan used to do?"

Erica nodded. "I'm not sure what I was hoping you'd say, but the murder put me right back in the room when I was investigating your brother's case. I know he's behind bars and it's impossible that he's responsible, but I wondered if you'd been contacted by anyone, perhaps someone who was paying a particular interest in his murders."

A strange expression crossed Lara's face, and she gave a choked laugh. "Contacted by anyone? Yes, I guess you could say that." Lara got to her feet. "Can I show you something, Detective?"

She got up to join her. "Yes, and call me Erica, please."

Lara led her out of the room and to the front of the house. Erica wondered if she was about to be asked to leave, but instead, Lara opened the door and walked out as well, and then turned to look up at the property. Erica joined her.

"Do you see how all the paintwork across the house and the front door is all different shades?" Lara asked.

Erica hadn't noticed it when she'd first arrived—she'd only observed the general tiredness and air of neglect that hung around the place—but now it was pointed out to her, she could see where the white stippled paintwork on the front had been painted over several times. The whole of the front hadn't been done, but instead it had been done in streaks and blobs, as though only parts had been painted over. The same thing applied to the dark-blue front door.

"Yes, I see it."

Lara approached the green wheelie bin that was placed to the left of the front door and pulled it out slightly to reveal a couple of cans of external paint. "I keep them out here because I need them so often."

Erica frowned. "I don't understand."

She sighed. "Detective, how do you think people reacted to knowing a murderer lived here, and that his sister still does? You asked if anyone had paid particular interest in his murders, well, this is the evidence I'm showing you. Lots of people paid attention, and they liked to remind me of that by spray-painting insults across the front of the house. Many of them weren't even to do with the murders and instead were directed at me, accusing me of"—her cheeks flushed crimson with shame—"having an *unnatural* relationship with my brother because of the paintings."

"You should have called the police," Erica said.

"I did. Many times. I called them when I had dog shit shoved through my letter box, too, and when someone threw a brick through my window, but other than coming around and filing a report, nothing was done." She pointed up to security cameras mounted on the walls. "They recommended I put those things up, which I did, but all that happened was the bastards spray-painted the front of the camera. They stand in a spot where they can't be seen by it and reach around with a spray can. Then they're free to do whatever they want. I took it down and cleaned the paint off the first few times, but then I figured what was the point, so I just left it."

"You haven't been tempted to move?"

A glint sharpened Lara's eye as she twisted to Erica. "Why should I? I didn't do anything wrong, except love my brother. All I ever tried to do was be a good sister, even when he controlled me. This just feels like another way of people controlling me, and I'll be honest, Detective, I'm pretty fucking sick of it."

This was a new side of Lara that Erica hadn't seen before. Was it possible to go through something as traumatic as she had and come out of it a stronger person? What Lara had learnt about her brother, plus the years of psychological torture he'd put her through, would have been enough to break the strongest of people, and yet here was Lara Maher ready for the fight.

"I'm not surprised. And no, I don't expect you to move. You're right, this is your home."

Lara's shoulders sagged, and she nodded and then turned and headed back into the house. Erica followed.

"Anyway," Lara said as she walked, "I kept everything for the police, in the hope that they might actually catch whoever has been doing all of this, so I guess you might as well take it. People liked to write me abusive letters that were put through the letter box, though I've taped it all up now, so I haven't had anything recently. There might be something there that will help you, though."

"Thanks. I'll definitely take them and have a look through. Even if it has nothing to do with this case, I might be able to nail the person down for you."

DCI Gibbs wouldn't want her distracted by a matter of harassment when they were working on a murder case, but Erica couldn't help but feel as though she owed it to Lara not to just let things rest.

"I'd appreciate that, though I'm not going to get my hopes up. I'm pretty sure that even if you found one of them, someone else would quickly take their place."

She didn't give Erica a chance to reply, but instead vanished into the kitchen. She returned a few moments later holding a plastic folder filled with pieces of paper.

"Here," she said, handing it to Erica. "I touched the first couple that arrived because I didn't know what they were, but once I'd realised, I used gloves to pick them up. I haven't read them, I just stuffed them in here in case one day the police might actually take an interest."

Erica offered her a smile. "I'm taking an interest."

"Shame it took another woman to die for that to happen."

"Yes, you're right. I'm sorry about that." Erica held up the folder. "Thanks again for these. I'll make sure I put some time into them."

Lara showed Erica out of the door, and Erica made her way to her car. She had a sick sense of unease in her chest, that feeling something was wrong and she'd let someone down. She didn't really think there would be anything in what she assumed was just hate mail in the folder, but she'd made a promise to Lara that she'd go through it and she intended to keep that promise.

Chapter Fifteen

After Erica had left Lara Maher's house, she headed back into the office. It had been another hour before Robert Day's solicitor finally bothered to show his face, and by the time they'd ended the interview and taken DNA samples and fingerprints, the afternoon had vanished. They'd be keeping Mr Day at the station until SOCO had finished going over his flat, and once that was done, he'd be free to return.

When her sister phoned to say she couldn't collect Poppy from school because one of her kids had come down with a sickness bug, it felt like just another thing had landed in her lap. The thought filled her with guilt. She shouldn't feel that way about picking up her own daughter—Poppy was her responsibility, not Natasha's—but she hadn't even had a chance to look at the letters Lara had given her yet, and she wanted to discuss her thoughts with Shawn, too.

"Hey, do you fancy a drive?" she asked him. "I have to get Poppy from school. One of Natasha's kids isn't well, and she thinks it's probably best if we're not over there tonight, so I'm going to have to take care of Poppy. I've got something to run by you, though, if that's okay."

He arched an eyebrow. "To do with the case?"

"Not exactly. I'm not sure what to do with it, to be honest. It would be good to get your opinion."

"Whatever you need."

They drove the twenty minutes to Poppy's school. As always, at this time of day, both the traffic and parking was terrible. But neither of them were parking wardens, so Erica just pulled into the first spot she saw—even though it was partly on double yellow lines—and jumped out of the car.

"I'll be right back," she told Shawn.

"No problem."

She was already running late so picked up her pace. She noticed a couple of the other parents had already collected their children and were now walking back down from school.

"Shit," she muttered to herself, but was rewarded with the glare of a mother who dragged her son along by his hand and had clearly overheard. Erica held herself back from repeating the word.

Poppy was already lined up inside the school gate waiting for her.

"Mummy!" Her whole face brightened at the sight of Erica. "Where's Aunty Tasha?"

"Ethan came down with a stomach bug, so you've got me tonight."

"Did you bring me a snack?"

Damn, she knew she'd forget something. Natasha would never forget to bring a snack when she was doing pickup. "No, sorry, sweetie. I didn't get the chance to get anything, but I'll get you something as soon as we get home, okay?"

"Don't you have to work?"

"Maybe a little, but I'll have to work from home. I've got someone waiting in the car for you, too."

Erica thanked the teacher and took her daughter's hand. Poppy shoved her lunchbox, coat, and school bag into Erica's other hand.

"I think you can carry something," Erica said. "You can at least wear your coat."

She hooked the hood over the back of Poppy's head, so she wore it as a cape and Poppy laughed.

Back at the car, Shawn was standing outside, the passenger door open, with him propped up against it. In his suit, he made for a striking figure, and she found herself smiling.

"Shawn!" Poppy broke free from Erica's grip and raced down the pavement towards him.

"Hi Popsy-Pops." Shawn caught the little girl under the arms and swung her off her feet. "How are you today?"

She squealed with laughter until he put her down.

"My name's not Popsy-Pops," she protested.

"Isn't it? Polly-Poppet, then?"

Poppy giggled. "Nooo!"

He cocked an eyebrow and twisted his lips. "Peggy-Pop-It?"

"You're being silly."

He ruffled her hair. "Would I ever do that?"

She put her hands on her hips and nodded determinedly. "Yes, all the time."

"Hmm, maybe you're right."

Erica laughed as well. "Come on, you two. Are we going home, or what?"

"Yeah! I want my snack."

Erica rolled her eyes. "Always thinking about your stomach."

She strapped Poppy into her car seat while Shawn got back into the passenger seat, then she drove home. Traffic was bad due to all the schools kicking out, so it took longer than normal, but Poppy chattered away the entire time so it didn't matter. Some kids were shattered by the time they finished school, but Poppy always seemed to go the opposite way and was hyper after a busy day.

Erica pulled up onto her drive, and they all climbed out. Poppy carried on with her stream of consciousness, standing right in the way as she told Shawn all about things other children he'd never even met before had done at school.

He held out both hands. "Wow, slow down, Poppy. Remember to take a breath."

"I'm taking a breath. Look." She sucked in a lungful of air.

"Okay, okay. Don't forget to breathe out again." He grinned. "Now are we going to go inside, or not?"

"Yes, let poor Shawn in, Poppy." Erica laughed.

Poppy jumped back and then did a dramatic bow like a courtier to a member of royalty.

"Cheeky monkey," Shawn said as he passed.

"I need to talk to Shawn about boring work stuff," Erica told her daughter. "You want to go and watch some television for a bit?"

"Do I get my snack?" Her eyes were bright. Poppy might only be seven going on eight, but she knew exactly how to work a situation.

"Fine, you can have some crisps, but just this once, okay?"

Both of them knew it was never going to be just the once.

Poppy clapped. "Yay, thank you."

Erica got Poppy settled in front of some terrible cartoon on the television. She was grateful Poppy hadn't yet discovered the joys of YouTube, though she'd mentioned it a few times when she'd come back from spending time at Natasha's house. Her cousins liked to watch annoying YouTubers doing annoying things—unpackaging toys, or playing computer games, or doing mindless challenges. Erica dreaded the day arriving when Poppy decided they were more entertaining than normal TV.

That made her think of the victim, Naomi Conrad. She'd made her living from that site and others like it. Had it also been what had got her killed? Right now, it was impossible to say.

She went back to Shawn in the kitchen.

"Drink?" she asked him.

"Sure, I could use a beer, if you have one."

"Absolutely." She took a couple of bottles from the fridge and cracked the lids off. She handed him one. They clinked the necks together, and she lifted the neck to her lips and took a gulp, the liquid cold and fizzy.

"So, what is it you've got to show me," Shawn asked after taking a swig of his own beer.

Confession time. "I went to see Lara Maher."

He raised his eyebrows. "Lara Maher, as in Tristan Maher's sister?"

"That's right."

"Why? I thought Gibbs said it wasn't worth following up."

"I know he did, but I just kept feeling like Naomi Conrad's murder was too similar to the ones Tristan Maher carried out."

"Why would speaking to Lara help? Her brother is in prison. It's not as though she would know anything."

Erica sighed, her shoulders dropping. "I know that."

"You don't think she might be involved, do you?"

She waved the beer bottle. "No, not at all. I don't know why I thought she'd know anything about Naomi—it's not as though they were connected in any way. The thing is, Lara has been having a pretty rough time of things. She's stayed in that damned house, and of course, everyone in the area knows what her brother did. She's been receiving hate mail, and people have been graffitiing the house."

"Did she report it?"

"Yes, but other than taking a statement, no one has done anything."

"How did it feel going back in that house?" Shawn asked, frowning.

"Weird. I don't know how Lara can stand to stay there, but she says it was her parents' house and it felt like deserting them if she sold or moved. She's still in contact with her brother. She writes to him, but she doesn't read his letters, or at least that's what she told me."

"I wish you'd said you were going back there. I'd have come with you. I don't like the idea of you being back in that house on your own after what almost happened."

"The house didn't do anything. Tristan is behind bars. I was perfectly safe."

A muscle in his jaw ticked, and his hand tightened around the beer bottle. "Even so, I don't like it."

Erica couldn't help smiling. "Are you about to go all alpha-male on me, Shawn? You know I'm more than capable of looking after myself."

His lips thinned disapprovingly. "Hmm. I'm not so sure about that."

"I'm not the one who ended up in hospital with a stab wound not so long ago," she pointed out.

"All right, it's not a competition." He was teasing her now, and the mood lightened a fraction.

She smiled. "Anyway, Lara gave me a folder of letters that she'd had pushed through her door. I haven't opened the folder yet, but from what she's said, they're the threatening kind. I didn't know what to do with them, since they're not officially part of our investigation, and I can't imagine Gibbs would be happy if I tried to bring them in. I didn't know Lara was going to give me something like this—I'd just planned on popping in for a chat, that was all."

"Let's take a look at them then."

"Here," she said, handing him a pair of gloves and slipping on a pair herself. "Just in case."

She opened the folder and took out the first of the letters. It was folded, so she spread it out. It was short and not terribly sweet.

Brother Fucker. Get out of our neighbourhood, you sick bitch.

Erica put it to one side and opened the next one.

You helped kill those girls. How could you not know? Lara and Tristan Maher will burn in hell.

Erica opened another letter, and another, and kept reading. Most of them had a similar tone.

Shawn blew out a breath and shook his head. "Jesus. How could she stay there on her own when she was getting all this abuse? She must be terrified knowing they all know where she lives."

The strange thing was, Lara hadn't seemed particularly afraid. Tired, maybe. More than tired. Weary, exhausted.

"She'd lived with Tristan her whole life, while he'd controlled and abused her. Perhaps, after that, living alone, even with all the threatening letters and the graffiti, still felt like a better option." Erica shrugged. "You'd think going through something like that would make someone weaker, but perhaps in Lara's case it made her stronger? She took on Tristan, and a few letters are nothing compared with him."

"You could be right." He looked down at the letters again. "I'm not sure what we're supposed to do with all these, though?"

"No, me neither. She put security cameras up, but they just spray-painted them, so she didn't get any footage."

"We're not going to figure out who sent these just from the letters. We can try to get some prints off them, but that's going to mean submitting them and the paperwork that comes with it."

Erica chewed at her lower lip and stared down at the hateful words scrawled across the pages. "I feel like I might have to do that, and deal with Gibbs when the time comes. I made a promise to Lara, and if there's a possibility we can nail one of the people who are doing this, it would send out a message to the others that they won't get away with it."

"You think it's more than one person?"

"Most likely, yes. There was a lot of media coverage of the case, and the press didn't exactly portray Lara in a good light. Plenty of them hinted that she'd helped her brother pick out his victims."

Shawn shook his head. "There was never any proof in that. She'd lived under her brother's coercive control her entire life."

"I know. That she'd sat for his paintings didn't look good on her either. Some of the portraits were leaked. Some people were more upset by a brother painting his sister naked than they were about the brother murdering innocent women."

"What is it about sex that upsets people so much?"

Erica shrugged. "The crazy thing is that it never was about sex. He never laid a finger on her, or so she says. He genuinely was just practising his art. He was good as well. He could have had a good career ahead of him."

"If he wasn't a murderous motherfucker, you mean?"

Erica smirked and glanced towards the kitchen door in the hope that Poppy hadn't overheard the swearing. "Well, yes, if it wasn't for that."

They grinned at each other. The kitchen door opened, and quickly, Erica gathered the letters and put them back inside the plastic folder.

"Mummy, I finished my crisps," Poppy moaned. "Can I have something else?"

"Absolutely not. You were lucky to get them, and I need to start dinner in a minute."

"But Shawn is here. I shouldn't have to go to bed when Shawn is here."

Shawn pushed his chair back and got to his feet. "Sorry, kiddo. I was only here to help your mum with a work thing. I'm not staying."

Her lower lip stuck out. "Not fair."

Shawn jerked his chin at the folder. "Do you want me to send those to forensics? I can do that now. I'm happy to take on the paperwork."

"You sure?"

"Yeah, I'm sure."

"Thanks, Shawn. I appreciate your help."

He ducked his head in a nod. "Anytime, you know that."

She did. He wasn't just a colleague, he was one of her closest friends as well, plus he was good with Poppy. Her daughter always got excited when Shawn came around. It must be hard for Poppy as well, not having her father in her life. She had her uncle, but he wasn't around a whole lot—Natasha did the vast quantity of parenting in their family. It wasn't that Erica wanted to replace Chris, just the thought tightened her chest, but she felt good when Shawn was around. There was a line she couldn't bring herself to cross, though, and that wasn't only because of her grief for Chris or her ongoing sense of betraying her dead husband. She and Shawn worked well as a team, and her work was the one place where she felt she had control. If something happened to mess that up, she didn't know what she would do. While she had her little family at home, her work family were just as important. They were a solid unit, and she didn't want to do anything to jeopardise that security.

"Say goodbye to Shawn."

"Bye, Shawn," Poppy said, obedient for once.

"Bye, Popsy," he teased.

Poppy stuck out her tongue and then scurried up the stairs, and Erica saw Shawn to the front door.

Chapter Sixteen
Three Months Earlier

Nicholas had received another letter.

They didn't arrive often—only one every few months or so. The content of the letters still didn't make any sense to him. They talked of things that he had no interest in such as bird-watching and oil painting. Nicholas still believed that whoever was writing to him had the wrong prisoner even though Nicholas's prison number was written on the envelope. He wondered if perhaps one day his pen pal would decide to pay him a visit and come to the prison in person. If that happened, he was quickly going to discover that he'd been writing to the wrong man all this time.

The idea of the letters stopping made Nicholas sad in a way he couldn't quite voice. Prison life was incredibly lonely. He'd believed he was used to loneliness. After all, hadn't he been alone most of his life? But, in the outside world, there were distractions. He'd even had a job working in that old people's home—the same one the detective's dad had ended up in. What a curious twist of fate that had been.

Perhaps people would think him strange, but he'd enjoyed the job. It had been the one place where others hadn't looked down on him. The residents had been more than happy to exchange a few kind words with him and had appreciated when he'd taken time out of his day to speak with them. Like him, many of them were the population's forgotten people, the ones who were ignored, who were put away so their family didn't have to think about them.

The detective hadn't been like that with her dad, he'd noted. Whatever else he'd thought of her, Nicholas couldn't deny that she'd gone in to see him practically every day. She had listened to what he had to say and not just dismissed him as being old and senile. But seeing that kinder side to her hadn't been enough for Nicholas to change his mind. She'd signed her death warrant the day she'd allowed his brother to jump in front of that train, and nothing would have changed Nicholas's mind on that.

He pulled his thoughts from the past and focused on the letter in his hand. Just like with all the previous letters, the envelope had already been opened, the contents checked by a drug detection machine. Paper letters could be sprayed with drugs like spice, which was almost impossible to detect by the naked eye, and the paper was then used to roll cigarettes. Paintings sent in by children could also be used to hide drugs inside of—not that anyone sent anything like that to Nicholas. His letters appeared innocent, and he doubted any of the officers really cared what was being said. After all, there were a thousand prisoners in here, and that meant there was a lot of mail to go through.

Nicholas unfolded the letter and started to read.

Dear Mr Bailey,

Is it easy to follow the passing seasons from inside those walls? It must be strange, being so cocooned from the rest of the world. Is cocooned the right word? It suggests that you are becoming something different while you're incarcerated. Are you? Spending years behind bars must change a man, I imagine. Of course, I'm just speculating—I've never spent any time in prison myself.

Anyway, I digress. I was talking about the seasons. One of the ways I've been able to tell that autumn is almost upon us is from the scent of bonfires on the air. Is it the falling leaves that encourages people to start their own little fires in their gardens, or is it the promise of Bonfire Night on the horizon?

Nicholas rolled from his back over to his stomach. He propped himself on his elbows, the letter on his pillow as he read.

Whatever the reason, I love the crackle and pop of a bonfire, and the scent of smoke on the air. Sometimes, I imagine the people gathered around them. The old man raking his leaves and garden clippings into the pile or children holding marshmallows or hot dogs over the flames. The smell of meat roasting on a hot flame is something to be savoured, isn't it? I always think the same when I walk past people having a BBQ. What about you, Nicholas? Do you like the smell of meat roasting? I wonder if there's something primal about it, like it takes us back to our ancestors' days as cavemen. Isn't that why men gather around a BBQ when those same men wouldn't be seen dead in a kitchen?

Back to you, Nicholas. Do you feel you're changing over your time spent inside? Like the creature inside a cocoon, or the shifting of seasons? Do you find yourself looking back over the things you've done and wishing you could have acted differently?

Perhaps there is still time?

Yours, M Cimi.

Did this M Cimi want him to repent? Was that his motive behind writing? He might be some religious nut who first planned to worm his way into Nicholas's life and win his trust before trying to convert him. It wouldn't surprise Nicholas at all. If anything, knowing something like that was going to happen made him feel a little better about the reason he'd been receiving the letters. There was a reason behind them, a reason he could understand. He didn't need to feel guilty thinking that he was reading letters that belonged to someone else or was writing back to someone who thought he was someone else. Not that Cimi had any chance of converting Nicholas. God or religion had never been present in his life, and he had no intention of going into it now. Some people in here, people who'd done terrible things, suddenly found God, as though it might make them a different person. Nicholas thought that was bullshit. Who you were didn't change just because you suddenly decided to believe in something that may or may not be real. That wasn't to say that Nicholas wouldn't go along with what Cimi wanted, however. He liked having someone to talk to, even if it was only through pen and paper. He could pretend to agree with his new pen pal, while knowing that he had no intention of ever finding God. How could someone like him ever find God? He didn't really believe in all of that, but if he did believe, he was fairly certain that when his time came, he'd be heading down instead of up.

Chapter Seventeen

Even though it was the weekend, Erica was back at work first thing the following morning.

Natasha's son was feeling better the next day, so Erica was able to drop Poppy off. She felt bad for being relieved that she was able to do so, but with such a big case on, she needed to work. It wasn't ideal that she hadn't been able to put in the hours last night due to childcare, though she had sat up at the kitchen table long after Poppy had fallen asleep and worked on her notes for both cases. She was lucky she had a boss who understood. It hadn't always been that way, but Gibbs had softened over the past couple of years, and they were less likely to butt heads now than they had been in the early days. Maybe it was just that she'd proven her worth over the years, or perhaps he simply liked and respected her more now. She knew his stroke had knocked his confidence, too, and while he was still perfectly capable of doing his job, she had noticed that he'd leaned on her a little more than normal. She didn't mind in the slightest. She liked to feel needed.

"Any updates with either case," she asked Rudd as she dropped her bag down beside her desk and hooked her jacket over the back of her chair.

"No new developments on the Skehan case, sorry."

"Shit. That seems to have gone cold already."

"I know. It's frustrating. There simply aren't any leads. No real witnesses, except for those who saw what happened *after* the attack, and nothing substantial from forensics. We don't even have anything on CCTV."

Erica released a breath. "It happens. As much as we'd like to catch the culprit in every case, sometimes we just don't. We just have to hope this is a one-off attack."

"Skehan himself hasn't been much help either. According to him, he doesn't have any enemies, no one he's fallen out with or who would want to hurt him."

"He seems like a nice enough bloke," Erica said. "He's on his own here. Family are in Ireland. No crazy ex-girlfriends who would pay to have someone disfigure him?"

"Nope. His story all checks out."

Erica twisted the wedding ring she still wore around on her finger. "What about the Conrad case. I hope we've had better luck there?"

"Digital Forensics are tracking down some trolls they've found via her social media accounts, ones who've sent her messages threatening to kill her or telling her to kill herself, that kind of thing."

Erica shook her head in dismay. "Jesus, what the hell is wrong with these people?"

"Makes them feel like they're important, I guess, to hide behind a computer screen and make some young woman feel bad about themselves."

It hadn't been words written on a screen that had harmed Naomi Conrad in the end. It had been a very real-life man with his hands around her throat.

"What about CCTV from her street?" Erica asked.

"Good news on that one, boss. We have a neighbour who has a Ring doorbell. We've requested the footage, and I'll send it over to you as soon as it comes in."

"Excellent. It would be good to find something that will back up Robert Day's story of another man arriving at her building as he was leaving. Right now, all we've got is his word for it, and considering the amount of his DNA at the crime scene, his word doesn't count for much."

"We've interviewed all the other residents in the block of flats, and no one else saw anyone coming and going at the time. Trouble is," Rudd shrugged, "it was the early hours of the morning, and people were in bed."

"Not everyone was in bed," Erica pointed out. "One man was leaving someone's bed. We just don't know if the woman whose bed he left was still alive when he did so."

"Even if we get proof that someone else entered the building after Robert Day left, we don't know for sure that he even went up to Naomi's flat. He could have been there for someone else."

"None of the other residents had visitors after midnight on the night she was killed, according to their statements, and they were all either home that night, or they weren't there at all." Erica twisted her lips. "If someone did arrive at the building, they didn't go to any of the other flats."

"Let's hope we can get the other person on camera then. If we can make an ID we could finally have a solid lead to go on."

"Let me know as soon as the footage comes in."

Her phone rang, and she nodded to Rudd to tell her they were done, and then answered it. "DI Swift."

A familiar voice came down the line. "Hi, it's Keith Allen."

She sat back. "Hi, Keith, how are you?"

"Not bad, not bad. I've just uploaded the results from the Conrad murder, but I thought I'd give you a call, as well, see if there's anything you'd like to talk through."

"Thanks for doing that. What did you find?"

She didn't have a problem getting results back via the computer, but she would always prefer to have a conversation with someone rather than everything being done by email. Maybe she was already old school at the grand old age of thirty-six, but she thought the current generation growing up was in danger of losing the art of having an actual conversation. Everything was done by text or messenger, or via social media.

"We've put the victim's time of death as being between midnight and three a.m. on the Wednesday morning. We found DNA beneath the victim's nails, which has been matched to Robert Day. The semen in the condom is also Robert Day's."

Erica rubbed the crook of her forefinger across her lips as she thought. "He admits to being there, but I really don't think it was him. Leaving a condom full of his DNA wouldn't have been the smartest move if he is the killer, but it might also be a double bluff. Unless he's an exceptional actor, he seemed too upset about her death, and the news came as a shock to him."

"Plenty of psychopaths and sociopaths seem like perfectly normal people on the surface," Keith said, "they're even charming. A lot of people who would consider themselves good judges of character have been taken in by them."

"I know, but Robbie Day doesn't seem like a psychopath or a sociopath."

He gave a small laugh. "There's the catch."

"What else did you find?"

"Fibres on the body. Some were from the bedsheets. The others are unknown. There was also saliva on the body that matched Robert Day."

"As I already said, Mr Day has admitted to being there the night Naomi died and says they had sex. Unless you were able to get fingerprints from the skin around her throat where the bruises are where she was strangled, I'm afraid it doesn't prove much."

"I wish I could tell you we could. The body looked like an attempt had been made to clean her after she was killed, but obviously, with the DNA beneath the nails, the killer didn't do a great job. It wasn't as though he put her in the bathtub or anything. I'd say it's more likely he wiped her down with a wet towel or something similar."

"Had a flannel or towel been found at the crime scene? There had been towels in the bathroom, of course, but could one of them have been used to clean the body? If so, have they been processed for DNA?"

"Yes, I believe so, but nothing other than the victim's DNA was found."

"He might have taken it with him as a souvenir then."

"Or he wore gloves," Keith suggested.

"But the towel or cloth would have picked up Robert Day's DNA if they had sex shortly before she was murdered. His DNA would have been all over her body and so it would make sense that it would end up all over whatever her killer cleaned her up with as well. So, if we found the cloth, it wouldn't just have had the victim's DNA." The certainty that he'd have taken it with him as a memento solidified inside her. Had Tristan Maher done the same with his victims?

She'd need to go back over the old case file to be sure, but she didn't think so. His souvenirs had been in the way of the photographs he'd used to paint his victims' portraits.

Why did her thoughts keep going back to that previous case? Other than the victim being strangled and left on the bed, naked, and the hair covering the bruising around the neck, there wasn't anything else linking them. And the person who'd murdered those previous women was currently behind bars and would be for the rest of his life. There was no possibility of Maher being responsible.

Could it be a copycat killer? If so, they'd got plenty of the details wrong, but then the police had never revealed everything to the public, even after Maher was put behind bars. She hoped more bodies weren't going to show up.

Shawn was working at his desk, so she got up and went over to him. He glanced up as she approached.

"Did you ever manage to look up the name of the man who came forward in the Maher case?"

He nodded. "Yes, I've got it right here. His name was Aaran Dunsted."

"Aaran Dunsted," she repeated. "That's right. I remember now. Creepy son of a bitch."

Shawn gave a wry smile. "That's the one."

"Have we got a recent address for him?"

"Yes. He's moved since we last spoke to him, but he's still local."

"Good. Let's go and have a chat. Find out where he was in the early hours of Wednesday morning."

Chapter Eighteen

Aaron Dunsted—the man who'd wrongly confessed to murdering two women, Emma Wilcox and Kerry Norris, a couple of years ago had downgraded from the already-crappy high-rise flat they'd searched during their investigations and was now living in a grotty single-room bedsit in Newham, East London. This part of London had one of the worst crime rates, double that of the national average. Unfortunately, crime came hand in hand with poverty. The high street was lined with pawnbrokers, Poundlands, and cheap fried chicken shops.

Dunsted's new place was a couple of roads back from the main road. Erica pressed the buzzer that had his name next to it. A moment later, he opened the door.

He hadn't changed much from two years earlier—the same wire-framed glasses and crucifix around his neck. Was that to lull people into a false sense of security around him? That, combined with the boyish good looks and posh accent, could easily lure a woman into believing he wasn't the type of person who got a kick from pretending he'd murdered two women. His light-brown curly hair was a little longer, but that was the only thing that hinted at the two years that had passed since she'd last seen him.

"Hello, Aaron," she said. "Remember me?"

It took a moment for a flicker of recognition to light on his face, but as it did, it was joined by a smile. "DI Swift, of course. How could I ever forget?"

His line of sight drifted past her shoulder to where Shawn stood. "And your partner is here, too. To what do I honour this reunion?"

"We'd like to come in for a chat, if that's all right?"

He glanced over his shoulder. "It's not really suitable for visitors right now."

"We won't judge." She paused and then added, "Unless you'd rather go down to the station?"

He huffed out a breath. "You'd better come in then."

Several doors led off the entrance hall, each one the entrance to a separate bedsit. A hole had been punched or kicked in the plasterboard wall and the carpet—if it could pass for a carpet—was stained and threadbare.

Aaron stopped at the first door and pushed it open. Erica and Shawn followed him inside.

A stale whiff of damp and body odour permeated the air, and Erica did her best not to wrinkle her nose. The room wasn't much to write home about. Other than a bed, there was hardly any other furniture. The single bed hadn't been made, the duvet twisted and hanging off the end. Dirty clothing lay in piles on the floor, together with used cups and plates stacked on top of one another. A small kitchen setup was in the corner, consisting of an electric hob, a microwave, a kettle, and a toaster. Another door opened onto the tiniest bathroom Erica had ever seen—a shower, a toilet, and sink crammed into what could have been a cupboard. She was relieved the walls weren't covered with newspaper clippings, as they had been in his previous flat. She remembered the walls plastered with articles about the women's murders and her previous cases, including Chris's death.

There was nowhere for them to sit, so they both hovered awkwardly near the door, while Aaron perched on the edge of the bed.

Erica looked around the room. "You used to work in graphic design, didn't you, Aaron? On the South Bank? I assume a job like that could afford you something better than this?"

His gaze shifted away. "I lost that job. Too much time in a psych ward didn't exactly enamour me to my employers."

"You can only blame yourself for that. We didn't come to you that time. You handed yourself over."

It wasn't unusual for them to deal with time wasters. They often had people saying they had information on a crime when they knew nothing. It was the same as when patients went into doctors' surgeries with made-up ailments just so they could talk to someone for a while. They craved the attention or sometimes were simply lonely.

He shrugged. "Doesn't matter. It was only a job, a job that bought things. Life's about more than just things, wouldn't you agree, Detective? It's *experiences* that are important. That's what we think about on our deathbeds, not our flat-screen televisions or our iPads or our fancy cars."

"True," she agreed, "but a good job is also an experience, as is the home we live in, or the food on our tables."

She wasn't here to discuss philosophy with him. "Where were you on Tuesday night, Aaron?" she asked, getting straight to the point. Her previous encounter with the man meant she had little time for him.

He frowned. "Tuesday? Right here, probably. I don't go out much these days."

"Can anyone else confirm that?"

"Why?" A slow smile curled his lips. "You think I killed that girl? The social media one?"

"We're just making some enquiries."

He gave a chuckle and rubbed his hand across his mouth. "Let me get this straight. You didn't believe me when I told you about the two other women, but now there's been another one, you're looking in my direction."

"We're simply covering all bases."

He huffed air through his nostrils. "It's kind of ironic, isn't it, that you come to me suspecting me of a crime when you didn't believe me when it was the other way around."

Erica folded her arms across her chest and resisted the urge to tap her foot. "It's not ironic, Aaron. We didn't believe you because you weren't the one to commit those crimes. The man responsible is behind bars."

He gestured with both hands. "Yet now there's been another woman murdered and you show up here."

"You showed a high level of interest in those previous cases, and this one is similar. We wouldn't be doing our jobs right if we didn't follow every lead, no matter how tenuous."

"I didn't kill that other woman, Detective. I'm over all of that."

His gaze was constantly fixed on Erica. It was as though he didn't even notice Shawn was in the room. He gave her the creeps, and she considered herself hard to shake.

"Over what?"

He gave a slow smile. "My obsession with true crime. I'm pursuing healthier interests now. Meditation and mindfulness."

Erica didn't believe that he'd simply stopped being interested. No one went from that level of obsession to nothing. With an internal shudder, she remembered how he'd become aroused when he'd lain in the spot where one of the women's bodies had been arranged.

"You still haven't answered my question. Can anyone confirm where you were on Tuesday night and the early hours of Wednesday morning?"

He pressed his finger to his lips. "Hmm. Let me consider my very full social calendar." He thought for a moment. "Wait a minute, on Tuesday I wasn't here. I mean, I was in this building, but I was down at one of the other residents' rooms, playing cards and having a few beers."

"You were with someone?" she checked. "Until what time?"

"Early hours. One-ish, I think. I didn't check the exact time."

The post-mortem report said that Naomi Conrad was killed somewhere between the hours of midnight and three a.m. Even if someone could confirm his whereabouts until one, that didn't rule him out. He still would have had time to murder Naomi.

"What's this person's name?" Erica asked.

"Troy. He's in number four. I don't know his surname."

"You don't know his surname?"

"No, it's not something I've ever asked. I doubt he knows mine either, unless he's been nosing at my post."

"I see." Erica glanced to Shawn, who returned her look with a slight nod. They weren't going to get anything else out of Aaron. "Okay, thanks for your time, Aaron. Hopefully, we won't have to be in touch."

Aaron got to his feet to show them out. "Thanks for the visit, Detective. Always good to know you're still thinking about me."

They left the building, the door shutting behind them. Erica paused on the doorstep, looking back at the property.

"If someone can confirm his whereabouts, he couldn't have been the one to murder Naomi," Shawn said.

"He said he was only with his neighbour until the early hours. Could he have had enough time to get to Naomi's flat and kill her after he'd left the neighbour's place?"

"Two hours to get to Naomi's flat and kill her?" Shawn raised his eyebrows. "Yeah, he had time."

Erica chewed her lower lip. "What about the time Robert Day says he saw someone going into the building? Could that have been Aaron? We could show Robert a photograph of Aaron and see if he can ID him?"

Shawn pursed his lips. "That's got all kinds of problems attached to it. Since we don't even know if Robert Day is innocent for sure, he could easily ID Aaron and shift the blame from himself."

"Not if we show him a lineup of photographs. If he picks Aaron out of numerous photos, we might be onto something."

"It's worth a shot, but we have no proof that Aaron had anything to do with Naomi Conrad's murder. All we're going on is that he had an obsession with two other murders a couple of years ago.

"Not just murders," Erica said. "Strangulations of young women in their beds. Aaron wanted for it to have been him to have done those crimes. Who's to say he hasn't gone a step further and done it for real this time."

"He has an alibi," Shawn reiterated. "We still need to check that out."

"Let's do it now."

The buzzer had the other man's name on it. Troy Sarty.

Erica pressed it. These weren't the posh kind with an intercom or a way to unlock the main door without physically getting up and doing it. The door swung open, and a young black man answered.

His gaze flicked up and down them. "You look like police."

"We are. Don't worry, you're not in any trouble. We just need to ask you a couple of questions about your neighbour, Aaran Dunsted."

His eyes narrowed. "What about him?"

She ignored the question and went with one of her own. "What's your name and date of birth?"

He rattled it off and Shawn jotted it down.

"Is this your permanent address?" Erica asked.

"Yeah, it is. Been here two years now."

"Do you live with anyone else?"

His eyes narrowed. "Nah, it's just me."

"When was the last time you saw Aaran Dunsted?"

Troy glanced over his shoulder, as though he thought he might find Aaron standing there, listening to what he had to say. "Umm, Tuesday, I think. Yeah, Tuesday."

"What time did he come over?" Erica asked.

"After nine. We had a few beers, played some cards, and hung out. No big deal."

"Was there anyone else with you?"

He pursed his lips. "Nope. Just the two of us."

"What time did he leave again?"

He shrugged. "Early hours. Was at least one. Might have even been two."

"And you played cards that whole time?"

"Yeah, pretty much. That's not against the law, is it?"

"Not at all. Thank you for your time."

He gave them a curious stare. "That's all?"

"Yes, that's all." She reached into her jacket pocket and took out a card. "If you think of anything unusual that happened that evening, though, please, do call us."

He took the card and then closed the door again.

Erica turned to Shawn. "Aaran's story seems to hold up."

"Yes, but it still doesn't mean he wasn't the one to kill her."

Erica gave a frustrated groan and rubbed her hand across her face. "Shit, I hate it when it feels like we're not getting anywhere."

"It's early days yet."

She shot him a sceptical look. "You know how much harder it is to catch someone the more time that passes. I already feel like I've failed Brandon Skehan. I don't think we're going to get anyone for what happened to him, either."

"You're being too hard on yourself. There isn't a single detective who exists who has solved one hundred percent of the cases they've been handed."

"I know. I just hate thinking that some son of a bitch is out there, laughing at us."

They got back to the car and ran both men's names for warrants and their criminal histories. Aaran Dunsted's history was already known to them, and it looked as though he'd mostly kept himself out of trouble since they'd last dealt with him. Troy Sarty had a handful of minor offences—low level shoplifting, driving without due care, and possession of controlled drugs. He had no kind of violent charges, though.

They drove back to the office. Erica grabbed coffee from the vending machine and went back to her desk.

"Boss, I've just sent the doorbell security camera footage over to you," Rudd called to her. "You might want to take a gander."

"Great, thanks."

Taking a sip of her coffee, she fired up her computer, logged on, and opened the file Rudd had uploaded. The camera gave a view across the street, from opposite Naomi Conrad's building. It was dark, but Erica could see the road at the front of Naomi's building, without actually being able to see the flats themselves. The streetlights were on, which helped a little, plus the owner of the camera had a security light on at the front of the house, but it was still night-time. Anyone who walked past the camera would appear as a silhouette.

She scrolled through the footage. Across the street, a taxi pulled up, and two people climbed out of the back. From their sizes and shapes, she could tell which was male and which was female.

Naomi Conrad?

It was impossible to know for sure, but she made a note of the taxi company, and checked the time. Eleven fifty-seven. The taxi firm should have a record of the drop off, and hopefully the driver would remember. The shadows of the couple's bodies merged as they drew each other in for a kiss. There was nothing about Naomi's body language that made Erica think she was in any way frightened of the person she was with.

The two of them vanished off-screen. Erica assumed they'd gone into the building, but, without any actual video footage of the front door, she couldn't prove it. Instead, she waited and kept watching. To save time, she increased the speed, slowing, pausing, and rewinding whenever there was movement on-screen—a car driving past, or someone on foot.

An hour passed, and then another. It was one-fifteen a.m. now.

Someone caught her attention. Instead of walking straight past, the person stopped on the other side of the street, as though they were waiting for someone, or perhaps even watching the building.

Erica froze the screen and squinted, leaning forwards. God, she was going to need to get her eyes tested soon. She was sure her vision wasn't as clear as it had been only a year ago. The figure looked like a man, from the height and the breadth of his shoulders. He was facing Naomi's building, so his back was to the camera.

Turn around, she willed him. *Come on. Turn around or just glance over your shoulder.*

It was all she needed, just a snapshot of a face.

Instead, something seemed to startle him, and he put his head down and his hands in his pockets and crossed the road, towards Naomi's building.

Erica hit 'pause' and checked the time again. One-twenty. Was that the time Robert Day had said he'd left? Had this stranger crossed the road because he'd spotted something through one of Naomi's windows and seen that Robert Day was leaving the building? Had he crossed the road to catch the front door before it swung shut again, locking him out?

If that was the version of events, then it meant Robert Day was telling the truth.

What had Naomi thought when someone had knocked on her flat door? Had she thought Robbie had changed his mind and had decided to stay the night instead? Had she opened the door with a teasing smile on her face, excited to have her lover back, only to have a stranger meet her instead? Erica imagined her trying to slam the door shut again, only for him to power through it, shoving her up against the wall and clamping his hand over her mouth to keep her quiet, before carefully shutting the door again.

If this was the person who'd killed Naomi Conrad, it took Aaran Dunsted out of the running. He wouldn't have been able to leave his card game and make it all the way here for this time. It was frustrating to have lost a possible suspect, but at the same time, she was relieved not to have to waste any more time looking into him.

Erica turned her attention back to the screen. The first man she'd been watching had vanished, but now she saw Robert Day crossing the road. He took out his phone and checked the screen and then headed off down the street.

The timings matched up to what Robert Day had told them in the interview. The question was, was Naomi Conrad still alive when he'd left?

Chapter Nineteen
Six Weeks Earlier

Dear Mr Bailey,

First of all, I want to thank you for your patience with my letters. I understand that they must be a little confusing. I hope this week my letter will bring some clarity to the reasons behind my fascination with certain species of wildlife.

There's one species that's caught my attention. These birds are only in the country for three months a year, arriving in early May and leaving in August. They nest in colonies in the eaves of old buildings, and they feed at higher elevations than the other birds they are sometimes mistaken for. Their closest relation is actually the hummingbird.

It's concerning me that these birds have stepped out of their boundaries. One bird in particular seems to think she is better than the rest. I believe you have experience of that, Nicholas? I have a plan to ensure this bird species stays within its territory. Perhaps it simply hasn't met the correct predator yet?

Perhaps it is time to visit the prison library to do some research on these matters? I look forward to hearing from you.

Yours, M Cimi.

Nicholas sat up and swung his legs off the side of the bunk, the letter still in his hand. He didn't know what it was his pen pal was talking about, but he sensed the importance in its tone. He was more than happy to do what Cimi had instructed in his letter. The library was somewhere Nicholas liked to be anyway. It was one place in the prison that tended to be peaceful. Of course, it didn't always stay that way—fights and arguments broke out just like anywhere else in this place.

They got one visit a week to the library, and his was coming up. He shifted around impatiently, the hours stretching ahead of him endlessly. Maybe he could get in the earlier group?

The tap of a prisoner officer's footsteps walking down the row of cells met his ears, and he jumped down from the bunk bed to be at the door to meet him. His heart sank when he saw it was Officer Bache, but he forced himself to stand tall. Those words meant something. His desire to understand what the letter meant was greater than his fear of the prison officer.

"Hey, boss, can I request a library visit to do some research? My slot is later, but I could do with going in the earlier group."

Bache stopped and eyed him suspiciously. "What do you need to do research on?"

"Just a bird species I'm interested in."

The prison officer stared at Nicholas as though he'd lost his mind. "What does the likes of you want with birds?"

Nicholas shrugged. "I like them. That's all."

He rolled his eyes. "Suit yourself. I think there's an empty spot in the earlier group. If I get you in, though, remember you owe me."

"I will, boss."

In the library, Nicholas didn't even know where to start. It wasn't as though he had never been in there, but he tended to just grab whatever was nearest on the shelf, rather than giving it any deliberate thought. Libraries hadn't been a place he'd spent much time at during childhood either. His mother had certainly never taken him to one—she'd been too busy getting drunk to worry about her sons' reading habits—and if he'd ever been to the one at school, it was only because he'd been forced to by the teachers, or else he'd been using it as a place to hide.

He stared around at the multiple shelves, trying to figure out where to start. Would they even have a book about birds in here?

A female voice caught his attention. "Can I help you?"

Officer Kebell. She was the Governor for Education in the prison. There weren't many women in here, understandably. He always found it a little strange that any woman would want to be around so many men, especially when they were mostly violent and hadn't had access to the opposite sex in quite some time. But there were female guards, and female volunteers as well. A lot of people saw education to be an important part of reform. Nicholas wasn't sure what good an education would do him. It wasn't as though he'd get out of here and go on to have a long and rewarding career. He knew his place in the world, he had since he was a small boy. He was pond scum, worthless, the lowest of the low. When he'd been teaching those who'd looked down on him, he'd finally felt like he was different, like he was strong and powerful and didn't have to play the role life had dealt him. But, after his experience in this prison, he'd come to finally accept that he would never be someone who had a special place in life. He was a nothing. A nobody.

This letter, though, that was different. Someone out there had chosen him. Had trusted him. Didn't that make him special?

Kebell was older than him, probably by a decade or more, but she was striking in a prim and proper way. Sharp blue eyes behind black-framed glasses. Red hair tied neatly into a bun at her nape. He'd never been interested in women. Why was this one affecting him?

"I'm...I'm..." he stuttered, not wanting to make eye contact with her. His cheeks burned, and he wished he could walk out of the building and pretend he'd never started this. But his need to find out what the letter meant was stronger than his embarrassment. "I want a book about Britain's native bird species. Would there be anything like that here?"

She gave a curt nod. "Of course. This way."

She led him down the corridors of bookshelves. He tried not to think about how her bottom filled out the uniform trousers, willing himself not to grow hard. He was already embarrassed; he would be mortified if she noticed. And the prison clothes didn't do much to disguise such things. Perhaps she was used to it, being around men all day. A wicked thought entered his head. Perhaps she *liked* it?

He clenched his fists and resisted the urge to hold them to his head and pound on his skull to get the thoughts out. He mustn't think like that. It was dangerous. Look at what had happened the last time he'd allowed dangerous thoughts to take over—he'd ended up in this place.

"Here we are." She drew to a halt and lifted her hand to run her finger along the spines of some of the books. She hesitated over one and then plucked it out from between its neighbours. "This should do it."

She handed the book out to Nicholas. He stared down at it dumbly. *The Complete Guide to British Birds.*

"Is ornithology something you've been interested in for long?"

He continued to stare at her. "Ornithology?"

"Yes, the study of birds."

That must be what Ornithology meant.

"I...I'm not. I mean, I like them. That's all. Like, if I went to the park, I'd sit and watch the birds."

"I imagine being in here can make you realise what you miss."

He nodded, not trusting himself to say anything clever. His tongue felt overly fat in his mouth, and his cheeks burned even more.

"Let's get it stamped out for you then," she said.

She used his prisoner number to mark the inside page of the book so the library service knew he'd been the one to check it out. He didn't plan on taking it back to his cell just yet, though. He would find a seat in the library and see what he could learn. He might need a different book, and then she could help him again.

Nicholas sat and unfolded the letter, placing it on the table beside the book. He read it through once more, making sure he hadn't missed anything. M Cimi was clearly describing a certain bird to him. It was Nicholas's job to figure out which bird he was talking about. He would have to read each page, hoping to recognise which it was. A bird that flew high and was only here a few months out of the year. A relation to the hummingbird. That ruled out lots of birds before he even needed to start reading. He knew it wasn't a sparrow or a crow or a blackbird, or any of the birds that were in the country all year around. And if it was related to a hummingbird, it would be small, like a robin, not a big bird like a swan or a bird of prey like a buzzard.

He flipped through the pages, ignoring the ones he knew didn't stand a chance of matching the descriptions and scanning those that might. He was painfully aware of the female officer's presence in the room, her exact location in relation to where he sat, and had to force himself to concentrate.

Turning the page, he flicked his gaze over the text.

High-flying bird. Only here over the summer months. Fed on insects.

And he suddenly understood what the letters meant. His heart rate ratcheted up a notch, and he sucked in a breath.

The bird his pen pal had been referring to was a swift.

Chapter Twenty

E rica's phone rang, and she answered. "DI Swift."

"Hi, it's DI Carlton from the Met Murder Squad."

"DI Carlton, what can I do for you?"

She knew Alex Carlton. He'd been involved in the Maher case as well.

"I'm phoning about a new case I'm on. I believe you might have an interest in it."

"I'm already running two big cases. How does your one involve me?"

Unfortunately, murders happened all over the city. Over one hundred every year, with even more deaths that would often end up being marked as death by misadventure or natural causes, but they still needed to be investigated. They had busy jobs.

"A body was found down near the Isle of Dogs."

"Okay," she said cautiously.

"The body had been burnt."

Erica's heartrate jumped. "Burnt?"

"Yes, doused with an accelerant and set on fire. Happened in the early hours, so no one was around to see it. The body was in a pretty bad state by the time the fire brigade got to it."

"You think it might be linked to the case I worked a few months back? Another case of people smuggling for black-market organs?"

"That's certainly one of the lines of enquiry I'll be following, but from the initial post-mortem it doesn't look as though organs had been removed."

"So, it might not be connected to the organ black market then. People still burn bodies to hide evidence."

Uneasiness coiled in her stomach. First the strangled woman and then this? Two crimes that seemed to be replicated from her past cases. Another thought hit her like a punch to the gut. What about Brandon Skehan. He'd been attacked in his home and almost blinded.

She wanted to shake the thought from her head. It was just a coincidence, wasn't it? Coincidences happen all time.

But ones like this? A woman strangled in her bed? A body burned? A man almost blinded? She was plagued by the uneasy sensation that her past cases were back to haunt her, but surely such a thing wasn't possible. She was being paranoid.

Carlton's voice brought her back to focus. "I'd like to see the files and have a chat with you about it, if that's all right. Compare notes."

"Makes sense. The location and disposal of the body is the same."

DI Carton was a good detective, though he was a little too sure of himself for Erica's liking. She imagined he was one of those men who thought if a woman was even in his vicinity, she probably fancied him. She sometimes caught him checking himself out in a car window mirror, doing an annoying pout and running his fingers through his hair. Yes, he was attractive, but there was nothing less attractive than a man who thought he was God's gift.

Still, she was a professional and would put her opinions to one side when it came to work matters. She wanted to find out if there were any other similarities to the black-market organ case she'd worked on not long ago. They'd put the ringleader behind bars, but experience told her that with that kind of trade, the leader was easily replaced. You cut one head off and another grew back in its place. It was incredibly frustrating, but that was how it worked when they created a gap in the market. No matter how many bad guys they took off the streets, while there was something people wanted or needed, and they couldn't get it the normal way, there would be someone who could offer it to them at the right price.

"I'm busy right now," she said, "but I can meet you somewhere for an hour, if you think it'll help."

"I do, thanks. Meet me down at the coroner's officer at four."

"It's a date," she said and then cringed at herself for the turn of phrase. She managed to hold herself back from trying to retract her words, aware it would only make her seem even more awkward than she already felt.

What was she hoping, or not hoping for? That the burning of the body had no relation to one of her previous cases, so she could get the idea that someone out there might be copying them, or that it did have to do with her previous cases so she could create a link and pull in the evidence from each of them.

Right now, she wasn't sure.

• • • •

DI CARLTON WAS WAITING in the car park. He saw her car pull in, took another drag from his cigarette, and then threw it to the ground. He crushed it beneath the heel of his shoe.

Was he going to pick up the butt? As a copper, he should know he needed to pick it up and dispose of it, but he probably thought those rules didn't apply to him.

Erica stopped the car and climbed out. "Those things will kill you."

"I know. I quit for six months and then fell off the bandwagon again. Everyone says it's alcohol and smoking that'll do it, but for me it was that early morning cup of coffee. Just never tasted the same unless I had a fag with it."

"We all have our vices," she said, offering him a smile.

"Do we, DI Swift? Care to share yours with me?"

"Too much fast food, an addiction to hot sauce, and an inability to separate my work and home life."

"Sounds like about ninety percent of the force."

"You got that right."

"Marry the force and get a divorce," he joked, but then he must have remembered how Erica's marriage had come to such an abrupt end and blood rushed to his face. "I mean, not for everyone."

"No, not for everyone." She cleared her throat and gestured to the front door. "Shall we do this then?"

"That's why we're here." He appeared relieved that she'd given him an easy get out. Would she ever get to a point where she didn't have how her husband had died hanging over her? People always seemed to feel like they had to pick their words carefully around her, in the same way an atheist might feel around someone who was highly religious—like they always thought the wrong thing was going to jump out of their mouths, unbidden.

John Hamilton was the pathologist working today. They went down to the basement, where the post-mortem examinations took place, to find him waiting for them. It would have been better if they'd been able to speak to Lucy Kim, since she'd done the examinations on Erica's previous case, but she wasn't in today. Erica hoped she'd be able to catch up with the other pathologist at some point and get her opinion.

"Do you have any idea who the victim is yet?"

"Not yet. There was no ID on or anywhere near the body. Once we get a better idea of their gender, age, and height, we can run it against our missing persons."

Both detectives put on protective outwear before entering. Photographs had been taken during the post-mortem and uploaded for them, but it was always helpful to see things in real life as well.

Erica believed she'd got used to the distinctive smell of a dead body, but a body that had also been burnt gave a whole new dimension to the aroma. She did her best not to show any discomfort. Having any form of an upset stomach always felt like a weakness.

"The body is female," Hamilton started, "and I'd estimate the age to be somewhere between eighteen and twenty-four. Height is about five-three, but again the pugilistic pose that burned victims end up in means I've made an estimate from the length of her bones. Time of death would have been sometime between midnight and six a.m., but that is harder to determine since the fire obviously has affected both the temperature of the body and the level of rigor mortis. Even though the body has become rigid, that's down to denaturation and coagulation of proteins rather than ATP depletion which causes rigor mortis."

"Was the burning the cause of death, or had they been killed before then?" DI Carlton asked.

This was his case, and though Erica was dying to ask what she viewed as being the most important of the questions, she forced herself to allow him to take the lead.

"There was no smoke in the lungs, so I'd say she was already dead when she was set fire to."

"Small mercy. So, what's the cause of death?"

"Strangulation. Though the skin is too damaged to show any bruises there is a hyoid bone fracture that is seen in about fifty percent of strangulations."

Erica looked at Carlton. "One of my other cases is also a strangulation. She was left in her bed, though, and wasn't burned."

"Unlike your previous case," he pointed out.

Should she confide in him that Naomi Conrad's strangulation also reminded her of a previous case? The hairs rose on her arms, her skin turning to goosebumps at the thought. She wanted to convince herself this was all a coincidence, but, aside from that it was DI Carlton and John Hamilton in the room with her instead of Shawn and Lucy Kim, she felt like she'd been propelled back in time.

Carlton must have noticed her shudder. "Everything all right there, Swift?"

She nodded. "Yeah, it's just weird how similar this is to my previous case."

"What else can you tell us about the victim?" Carlton asked the pathologist.

"I'd say whoever she is, she's led a hard life. The hyoid isn't the only bone that's fractured. Though the others are all healed, she has, at some point in her past, received two fractured ribs, and a fractured jawbone, and eye socket. She's also broken several of her fingers."

"That sounds like someone has been beating her," Erica said.

"Yes, and from the various points of healing, I'd say it's been over a period of time as well."

Carlton's brow furrowed in a frown. "Could she be an immigrant?"

The pathologist shrugged. "That's impossible for me to say at the moment."

"What about her organs?" Carlton asked. "Were there any missing?"

He shook his head. "No, from my examination, there doesn't appear to be any organs missing."

Erica glanced over at the other DI. "Then this isn't a black-market organ case."

He met her eye. "Is that what you were fearing?"

"Weren't you? It had all the traits of the case I covered a few months back."

"Except for the missing organ."

She chewed on her lower lip as she thought. "Maybe she was killed for another reason. If she's been beaten, and has been for some time, this might simply be a domestic abuse case. Perhaps whoever killed her had read about the other cases in a newspaper or online and used the same method to hide his own crime in the hope that we'd put it down to another black-market case."

"Then why not remove an organ at the same time?" Carlton said. "We would have been convinced then."

"Perhaps he didn't have the guts for it—no pun intended. If she was someone he thought he loved, no matter how badly he was treating her, he might not have been able to bring himself to cut her open. Punching and strangling someone in a fit of passion or anger is very different to getting a knife and deliberately cutting someone open."

Carlton gestured at the blackened shape on the table. "He had it in him to set her on fire."

"But again, that's something that can be done from a distance. Pour petrol on the body, light a match, and walk away."

He huffed out a breath of air. "So you don't think the same crime syndicate who were responsible for your previous case also did this?"

"No, I don't, sorry. I think you're looking for someone with different motives." She decided to tell him. "It is bothering me, though, that this case is so similar, at least on the surface."

He frowned at her. "Why?"

"Because I'm also dealing with another case that reminds me of one I've covered before. I want to tell myself this is a coincidence, but my gut is telling me otherwise."

"Cases can appear similar, once you've covered enough of them."

"But two in a row?"

"Technically," he said, "this is my case, not yours."

"True. I just wonder if there's anything, other than the strangulation, that might link this with the Naomi Conrad murder. Perhaps we could match DNA or clothing fibres that might tie them together?"

DI Carlton pursed his lips, and one eyebrow pulled down in a quizzical expression. He didn't seem convinced. "That sounds like a very tenuous link."

"You're probably right, but it would put my mind at rest."

John Hamilton cleared his throat. "I hate to throw a dampener over all this, but getting DNA off a burned body is almost impossible. The victim's bones are highly degraded so genetic markers are hard to amplify, and any DNA the killer might have left on the body would have been destroyed."

"Shit." She balled her fists and resisted stamping on the floor. She was going to need something more if she could prove her theory that this was linked.

"There we go then," Carlton said, "problem solved. Besides, running extra tests just because of some random idea that it's related to your case seems extreme. As far as I can see, there's no proof of that, and we're detectives, we work on proof and facts."

"They were both strangled," she pointed out. "Both women of approximately the same age. Both killed in the same area."

"Strangulation is a common murder method, especially in women."

She sighed. "Maybe you're right and it's just coincidence." She looked to the pathologist. "But will you keep an eye out for anything that might tie them together. I know it's hard with a burned body, but DNA or clothing fibres, or hairs that match both the bodies."

"Of course."

"And you'll let me know of any developments?" she asked Carlton.

"Yeah, I can do that. I'll expect the same in return, though."

She put her hands out either side of her. "Always happy to work together if it means finding out who was responsible for hurting these women. After all, we're on the same side."

Chapter Twenty-One

"You still here?" Erica said to Shawn as she got back to the office. "It's Saturday night. Don't you have somewhere more interesting to be?"

"Don't you?" he quipped back.

"Not really. Poppy's having a movie night with her cousins and will probably sleep over. She always falls asleep during a film. I'll only be going back to an empty house."

"I wanted to follow up some things," Shawn said. "While you were with DI Carlton, I tracked down the taxi company that Naomi Conrad used and spoke to the driver. He does remember dropping Naomi and a man off at her flat just before midnight on the night she died. I showed him a photograph of Robert Day, and he says it's the same man. We also have Robert on camera leaving Naomi's flat, so that matches his story, as does the arrival of another man at the same time."

"But we still don't know if Naomi was alive or dead when he left her."

"And we didn't catch the second man leaving the block of flats either. Unfortunately, the angle of the camera doesn't hit the front door, so he may well have left that way, but just stuck to the far side of the road."

"We know he was on foot, though," Erica said, "not that it helps us at all. What about forensics on the flat?"

He shook his head. "It was clean. No sign of the missing phone, and nothing in it that would suggest he murdered Naomi. There was nothing in any of the messages that the two of them sent each other that had any hint of violence or arguments either."

"So, no motive," she raised an eyebrow, "other than sex."

Shawn changed the subject. "How did it go with DI Carlton?"

"Okay, I think. I don't believe his case is linked to the black organ market, though he's not ruling out that line of enquiry. My money is on her being a domestic violence victim."

"No one's reported her missing yet?"

"Not as of yet, though Carlton has his team going through misper cases. The amount of burn damage to the body is severe, though, so, as we know from previous experiences, it's hard to make an ID."

Previous experiences being yet another similar case that had cropped up.

Erica caught Shawn staring at her.

"What?" she said.

"Something's bothering you, I can tell."

She perched on the edge of her desk. "Okay, you're right. I don't think the case is linked to the black market one, but I do think it's been staged to make it look like it might be. And here's the other thing, remember how I mentioned the Conrad case reminded me of the Maher case as well? That means it's two in a row now."

Shawn thought for a moment and then said, "What about the attack on Brandon Skehan?"

"What about it?"

"Someone went for his eyes, didn't they?"

A rush of cold drenched through her blood, and she sucked in a breath. Hearing Shawn confirm her suspicions suddenly made it real for her. "You don't think...?" She couldn't even bring herself to say it—to say *his* name.

"It's a possibility."

"I mentioned to DI Carlton that I thought our two cases might be linked, not only because it reminded me of the previous cases, but because both victims were of a similar age and both strangled. Is it possible there's a third case, and if so, what does it mean?"

Shawn put up both hands. "Hey, I might be completely wrong. It's a bit of a tenuous link. It wasn't as though Brandon Skehan was abducted or anything. Someone attacked him in his home."

"He fought back," Erica said. "Maybe the plan had been to abduct him and cut out his eyes, but the attacker didn't get the chance because Skehan escaped." She ran her hand over her face. "Shit, I don't know what to think. My head's all over the place with this. I don't want to be distracted by something that's only in my mind."

"Might be worth talking to the victim again with a different view point?" he suggested.

"Maybe that's what I'll be doing tonight then."

Shawn glanced at the clock on the wall. "Tonight? Don't you think you'd be better off getting some rest and coming back at it with a fresh head?"

She arched her eyebrows at him. "Who's the boss here?"

"Okay, okay." He grinned. "God forbid I ever attempt to tell the indomitable Erica Swift what to do."

Was she right in thinking the cases were all linked? There was a difference between a big crime scene like the organ black market, where multiple people in various cities and countries might be involved, and something on a much smaller scale like an attack on a man or woman in their home? She'd already told Shawn about the Naomi Conrad case reminding her of Tristan Maher, but at that point she hadn't considered the attack on Brandon being anything like the crimes Nicholas Bailey had committed two years ago.

Was it possible, though? If all three crimes were connected, there was one thing that made that connection.

Her.

• • • •

BRANDON SKEHAN OPENED the door and blinked in surprise. Well, his one good eye blinked in surprise—the injured one was still covered with the bandage. Could it have been that he was never meant to keep that eye? If his attacker had got his way, would Brandon have found not only that eye, but the other one, too, plucked from his head? She remembered her fear of that happening, how, when she'd woken in the dark in an abandoned underground station, and hadn't been able to see anything, she'd been certain it had already happened.

Nicholas Bailey had sedated his victims before he'd cut their eyes out and then released them to wander London's streets, newly blinded. If someone was trying to replicate her previous cases, why hadn't they sedated Brandon before they'd attacked him? Was it possible the attacker hadn't been aware of this piece of information? Just like an organ had never been taken from the body burnt down by the canal. The crimes weren't perfect replicas, but they were close enough.

"DI Swift. I wasn't expecting to see you again so soon. Do you have news for me?"

She could tell by the lift in his voice that he was hoping she'd say they'd caught his attacker, but she wasn't able to do that. "No, I'm sorry. Not exactly. I wanted to ask you a couple more questions, if that's all right."

"Yeah, sure. Come on in. I'd give you the tour, but I guess you've already seen the place."

"I have but thank you." Was he embarrassed that she'd poked around his home when he wasn't here? It would have felt invasive, to know strangers were poking around your belongings, even though they'd never searched through his personal things—they were only ever looking for evidence so they could find out who'd attacked him.

"It doesn't really feel like home anymore," he said, as though reading her thoughts. "Not because the police were in here, but more because it just doesn't feel safe now. I only rent the place. I've got a couple months left on the lease and then I'll move." He gave a rueful smile. "In fact, I might just say screw the deposit and leave sooner. Depends on how many more sleepless nights I can stand."

"You're not sleeping well?" she enquired.

"Bad dreams. Nightmares really. Seems like such a stupid thing to say, and I'm embarrassed to admit it. It's something you'd expect from a kid, not an almost thirty-year-old man. There are some nights I don't want to switch the light off."

"We all get nightmares, Brandon. It doesn't matter how old we get. And after going through something like you did, it's hardly surprising. You've probably got PTSD from the attack." She still had nightmares and it was two years later.

He gestured to her wedding ring. "I see you've got someone to go home to, at least. I think I'd feel safer if I wasn't on my own the whole time."

Automatically, her right hand moved to cover her left one, hiding the gold wedding band. "Oh, well, I don't really have anyone. I did. I was married. I still am married." She stumbled over her words. "He died a couple of years ago."

"Oh, shit. I'm so sorry."

"It's fine," she said, even though it wasn't. It was far from fine, but she didn't want to make anyone else uncomfortable because of her circumstances.

"How did he die?"

"It was sudden," she said. "Taken too young. Life can be cruel." She didn't want to give him any details. She hadn't lied exactly, but also hadn't told him the truth. She didn't want to tell a man who'd been attacked in his home that her own husband had been brutally murdered. What kind of confidence in her abilities would that give him, if she hadn't even been able to keep her husband safe?

He put up both hands and shook his head. "Sorry, I shouldn't pry. Ignore me."

She gave a tight smile. "Don't worry about it."

It would be easy enough for him to find out what had happened to her husband. All he needed to do was Google her name and numerous articles would come up. She hoped he wouldn't. She didn't want him to pity her or to think she was bad at her job.

She brought the topic back to the case.

"I'm sorry to make you go through this again, but I wanted to talk to you about the attack. I know you said it was dark and it happened fast, but I need some more details."

"Okay. What kind of details?"

"Your attacker slashed you across the face, but you said you moved when the knife was coming down. Is there any chance your movement also changed the direction of the knife?"

He frowned. "Changed the direction? I'm not sure what you mean?"

"Could the tip of the knife originally have been pointed down, in a stabbing motion, rather than a slicing?"

"You mean, did he try to stab one of my eyes out?"

She winced at the image that must have brought to mind. "Yes, I do."

He thought for a moment. "I guess so. When I lurched back, jerking my face away from the knife, he was behind me with that arm curled around my head. My shoulder would have struck his bicep and so could have changed how he was pointing the knife."

Erica nodded, picturing the scene in her head. That would make sense. Of course Brandon's movements would have affected those of his attacker.

"Why are you asking me all of this?" Brandon said, his frown deepening.

She couldn't give him too much information. "Just following a lead. There's the possibility whoever did this might have done something similar before." Even though he was currently serving several life sentences in prison.

Brandon straightened, his forehead smoothing, his blue eyes brightening. "That's good, isn't it? Not that they did this to someone before, but that you've got a lead."

She risked a smile, though she didn't feel it. How could she possibly explain to him that her so-called lead was someone who had been behind bars at the time of the attack? Brandon wanted her to make him feel better, to reassure him he was going to be safe in his own home, but she couldn't.

"I wish I could tell you that we'd already caught the bastard, but I'm sorry, I can't."

"It's okay. I know you're doing everything you can."

There was one thing that she had wondered about. Why hadn't Brandon put the light on the moment he'd stepped into the flat? She knew it was the first thing she'd do when she got home. The light switch was on the inside wall just past the door, so she'd open the door and flick the light on even before she'd really stepped into the house. Why hadn't Brandon Skehan done the same?

"One last question, Brandon, if that's all right?"

"Sure."

"Why didn't you put the light on when you got home? The witnesses who helped you right after the attack say the flat was in darkness, and you said yourself that you hadn't seen your attacker because it was dark. But it wasn't as though you had a power cut or anything, so why didn't you turn on the light?"

He shrugged. "There didn't seem to be much point. I was going to bed."

"You still had to find your way to your room. Wouldn't it have been easier to put a light on?"

"Maybe, but I was planning to use the bathroom first and I'd have put the light on in there. Detective, you've seen my flat. It's hardly on the large side. It's literally a few steps between the front door and the bathroom, so I would have just put the bathroom light on, had I reached it. It's really not a big deal."

She sighed. "I suppose I was just thinking that you might have seen the attacker if you'd put on the light, or at least might have noticed that something had been moved."

"Aye, I wish I had now, too, but to be honest, I'd had a few pints and I probably wouldn't have noticed anyway."

"Thank you." She got to her feet. "I'll leave you in peace now, but if you think of anything else, please do call me."

"I'll do that." He paused and then added, "Maybe, when you're free sometime, I could buy you a drink and you could give me some advice about how I can start thinking about joining the police, as well?"

Erica's insides jolted, and heat rose to her cheeks. He wanted to buy her a drink? Was this just an excuse for him to take her out, or was he genuinely wanting to know how to get into the Met? No, of course he didn't want to take her out. She was older than him, and a mother. He was an attractive bloke and could be out pulling hot twenty-one-year-olds. She was misreading this in completely the wrong way. She hated feeling so awkward, and like she was going to misstep the situation and look like an idiot. She was a professional woman.

"I'm afraid free time isn't something I have much of. You can find plenty of information online, though."

"Oh, right. No problem."

Now he was the awkward one, and she found herself feeling bad about that.

"Besides, it wouldn't be very ethical of me to go for a drink with a victim in a case I'm working on. The boss wouldn't approve."

"No, I totally understand. I didn't mean to put you in a difficult position. Perhaps you'll think about it once the case is over?"

Erica took a couple of steps towards the door. "I really should be going."

"Yes, of course. I'll show you out." He offered her a smile. "Sorry I made things weird."

Erica laughed. "No, it's fine, really. Thank you for your time."

"Anything I can do to help," he said and showed her out of the door.

Chapter Twenty-Two
One Month Earlier

Nicolas stood in line, waiting for his meal, his tray in hand. On the other side of the canteen, Officer Bache walked back and forth, his gaze fixed on the prisoners sitting at the tables, making sure each of them was eating quickly enough and not doing anything to break the rules.

The queue moved forward, and Nicholas wasn't fast enough to fill in the gap and received a fist in his back as thanks. He staggered and almost fell into the man in front but managed to keep to his feet. He immediately looked down at the tray, his shoulders rounded, his neck bent, taking on a submissive posture. Even a split second of eye contact with the wrong person in this place could mean a beating.

He shuffled on, waiting his turn in line until he reached the front. Rice and curry was slopped onto his plate, and he helped himself to a carton of juice and a bread roll.

With the tray in his hands, he moved up the far side of the canteen, searching for somewhere to sit. Officer Bache had seen him coming, and the prison officer's face crumpled into a scowl. Just like with the other prisoners, Bache could sense weakness, and it seemed to disgust him.

Nicholas kept going.

A foot stuck out from under one of the tables, catching Nicholas's ankle. To his horror, he flew forwards, and he automatically released the tray with one hand. The forward motion caused the tray to swing out to his right, and as his arms flew up, the edge of the tray connected with Officer Bache's face.

Curry and rice landed all over the prison officer, a red gash beneath his eye already forming where the tray had struck him.

Nicholas hit the floor, his teeth clacking together, the air bursting from his lungs. But he didn't even care about his own pain. He'd hit Officer Bache in the face with a tray and he knew this was going to get bad.

The canteen erupted in chaos. Shouts of encouragement were layered with warnings from the other officers.

A heavy body landed on his back, crushing what remained of his breath from his lungs. A knee planted painfully in his spine and jammed down, flattening him to the floor.

I'm sorry, he wanted to tell them. *It wasn't me. Someone tripped me. It was an accident.* But his breath was a painful, narrow wheeze, and the words refused to come. He tried to lift his head from the floor, but it was shoved back down again, his temple hitting the hard surface, a loud crack ricocheting through his ears.

The other inmates took in the sight of Officer Bache covered in Nicholas's curry and rice and peals of laughter echoed around the hall, but they didn't drown out the fury in Bache's voice.

"What do you think happens to an inmate who dares to assault a prison officer?"

Nicholas tried to speak but was rewarded with another boot in the spine.

Bache and another of the officers hauled Nicholas to his feet.

"I don't want to hear it," Bache snapped. "A few days in the box should sort you out."

"No, please."

He didn't want to go in there. He'd heard rumours. There was nothing in the room, except for a toilet—no bedding, no windows, nothing to distract his thoughts.

"Next time you'll think twice before trying something so stupid."

They dragged him out of the canteen, down the corridors, to the end where the box was located. One of the officers released him long enough to open the solid metal door, and then they threw Nicholas inside.

The moment the door slammed shut, a metallic clang echoing around the enclosed space, Nicholas was back on his feet. He threw himself at the shut door and battered his fists on the metal.

"I didn't do anything wrong! I don't deserve to be in here."

A muffled voice came from the other side of the door. "You assaulted a prison officer with a tray. You deserve to be in there for a very long time."

"No, wait!"

But footsteps clicked away, and Nicholas knew he was alone. Just as he would be, day after day, night after night, until they decided his punishment was over.

• • • •

TIME PASSED.

Nicholas slept and woke, and slept and woke again. With no barred window and a solid metal door, there was no movement of air in the cell, and it was hot and stuffy. He felt as though he'd been drugged, now living a strange existence of little to no routine, and barely any contact with another person.

"What are you doing, Nicholas?"

Nicholas jerked awake. He'd been dreaming. He must have been, but he would have sworn he'd heard his brother's voice, as clear as though Danny had spoken right into his ear.

"What—what?"

He flickered open his eyes, but it was dark. It must be night again. Other than the bells ringing through the prison, and the meals he was given through the hatch in the door, he had no way of telling the time of day. Normal prison life meant he was locked in his cell from six p.m. until eight a.m., but now he was in here twenty-four-seven.

"It looks like you're struggling in here."

Nicholas blinked into the darkness. "Danny?"

"Yeah, Danny. Who else is it going to be?"

He wanted to tell Danny that it couldn't be him, because his brother was dead, but, weirdly, he worried about pissing Danny off if he tried to argue with him.

"I said, it looks like you're struggling."

"I suppose I am." It suddenly felt good to be able to say it, and to have someone on his side, even if he knew that person wasn't real.

At first, when he'd been put behind bars, he'd experienced a kind of notoriety. The things he'd done had been plastered all over the media, and the other prisoners had treated him with respect. For the first time in his life, he hadn't felt like an outcast. Men had clapped him on the back and invited him to sit with them at mealtimes and listened to him regale the stories of the things he'd done—especially the one where he'd killed a detective's husband. That was one of their favourites. But it hadn't taken long for them to grow bored of the stories. Nicolas had been able to tell by the way their gazes drifted away when he started to talk and how they spoke over him or simply turned their backs to start conversations with someone else.

He'd felt it all slipping away, the respect, the notoriety. It had filled him with panic, and the harder he'd tried, the more he'd caught those disdainful glances and shrugged shoulders. He'd quickly returned to the nothing person he'd been all his life. No one noticed him, or if they did, it was for all the wrong reasons.

"You're being stupid, Nicholas," Danny said. "Did I teach you to be stupid?"

"No, Danny. You didn't."

"Why do you let them treat you like that?"

"It's not my fault. I don't have any choice." His voice was a hoarse whisper. He didn't want any of the other prisoners or officers to hear him. "What are you doing here?"

"I came to see you. Heard you were getting into a bit of trouble and I thought you could do with your brother's shoulder to lean on."

"You...you can't be here, because you're dead."

"There are some things you just need to accept that you won't understand. I'm here, aren't I? You can hear me, so I must be here."

Nicholas shook his head. "No, I must be imagining you."

Danny's tone changed. "You're hurting my feelings now, Nicholas. I make all this effort to come and see you, and that's how you treat me?"

"Sorry, Danny."

"You need to listen to me, okay, and you need to listen to me hard. You have something you can use, and you're not making the most of it."

Nicholas wrung his hands together. "I don't know what you're talking about."

"The letters you're receiving mean something. Someone has been contacting you for a reason, and I think you know what that reason is."

He spoke in a whisper. "He wants to kill the detective."

"Exactly. You have a fan, Nicholas, someone who wants to complete your work. What's more important to you, having him kill Erica Swift, or getting out of this place sooner?"

The seduction of both possibilities hung on the air. Which siren song was stronger?

He wanted Erica dead, didn't he?

"You can kill her," Danny's voice came out of the darkness. "If they let you out early, it can happen at your hands. You'll take your revenge for my death yourself."

But an uneasiness twisted Nicholas's stomach. "I've already made her pay, haven't I? I took her husband from her."

"And then she got you locked up in here. Do you think that's fair? Do you?"

Nicholas put his hands over his ears and rocked in the corner. "Don't shout at me, Danny. It's not my fault. It's not my fault. It's not my fault."

Nicholas had always been frightened of his brother's temper. He'd been frightened of almost everything when he'd been growing up. That was his resounding emotion when he thought back to his childhood—fear and shame. Their mother had always loved Danny more, even though she'd had a strange way of showing it. It wasn't that she'd been particularly loving with either of them, but whenever she'd got drunk and her anger had taken hold, it had always been Nicholas she'd made a beeline for. Perhaps she sensed the weakness in him, just like everyone else did. Danny had always been stronger, at least, until he hadn't. In the end, he'd gone the same way as their mother—too much drinking and drugs, letting the anger take over. Nicholas had done the same—not with the drinking and drugs, but with the anger—and look where that had got him.

He didn't know how long he stayed that way, with his hands clamped over his ears, rocking back and forth, but when he eventually lifted his head again, the lights were back on and his brother was gone.

Had he been right, though? Did all those letters he'd been receiving mean something important? He'd put the code together himself, hadn't he—the one about the bird? He'd known the letter-writer was talking about the detective. Could he really use them to get his sentence reduced?

More than anything, he hated being in this place. He was miserable. What was the point in going on if this was his life now? Those letters were a small beacon of hope. He'd thought he'd felt that way because it had been good to know that someone was thinking about him, and the letters broke up the mundanity of prison life, but perhaps they meant something more?

What would happen if he allowed this person to kill Erica Swift? Would the letters stop? Where would that leave him? Yes, the detective would be dead, but he'd still be facing a lifetime in prison, and maybe his letter-writer would have fulfilled his purpose and stop writing to him.

Then he'd be left with nothing.

. . . .

WHEN NICHOLAS EVENTUALLY got out of the box, weeks later, there was another letter waiting for him. It was short and to the point.

Dear Mr Bailey,

I've brought all these things together now, Nicholas. It's time I did a little exterminating of these beasts, those birds in particular, wouldn't you say? I've set a fire, and done some painting, among other hobbies I enjoy. Now it's time for the grand finale, to finish off the job you started.

Yours, M Cimi.

That evening, as Fish watched the television and the local news came on, Nicholas paid extra attention. The news reporter spoke of crimes that had happened across the city, and finally the penny dropped. He understood what those letters meant.

Nicholas made up his mind, but first there was something he needed to do. He gathered all the letters together and called for one of the prison officers.

Chapter Twenty-Three

Erica managed to spend Sunday with Poppy. They went for a walk to the park and fed the ducks. Erica even cooked a roast dinner, though sometimes it felt like a big effort just for the two of them. Poppy enjoyed the routine, though, sitting at the big table with placemats and a fizzy drink and a warm syrup sponge and ice cream for pudding. Then it was bath and hair-washing time, and before Erica could figure out what had happened to the day, it was time for bed again.

Monday morning arrived, and she braced herself for a stacked desk. Weekends were always busy, which invariably got shifted to Mondays.

Her phone rang, and she answered.

"Will you take a reverse charge call from Belmarsh Prison?"

It caught her completely off guard. Prison? Who would be calling her from there?

"Umm, yes, okay."

"Connecting you."

Her fingers tightened around the phone, her body bolt upright, every muscle tensed.

The male voice on the other end of the line sent shards of ice through her veins. "DI Swift?"

"Who is this?"

"Don't say you've forgotten me already, DI Swift."

All of a sudden, the bustling energy of the office and all her colleagues around her seemed to pull away, so they were distant and faded. The only thing that existed for her now was the phone and the person on the other end of the line.

"Nicholas Bailey? Is that you? Why are you calling me?"

"I have information that will help you."

"Information about what?"

"There have been cases, haven't there? Ones like before."

Her heart seemed to stop. "What?"

"Someone has been writing to me about them."

"Why do you think that, Mr Bailey?" Even speaking his name felt like poison on her tongue.

"Because they've been sending me letters describing certain...hobbies...and they match the cases you've investigated. There's going to be another one, and it'll be soon."

"How do you know that?"

"Not like this. I won't talk to you about it on the phone. You need to come and see me."

Her other hand balled into a fist. "You want me to visit you?"

"Yes, I do. And if you want to hear what I have to say, you'll do as I ask. Come alone, DI Swift. I'll refuse to see you, if you don't."

The line went dead, and Erica was left staring at the phone, her mind reeling. Had that really just happened?

From across the office, Shawn must have caught sight of her face. "Everything okay?"

"Nicholas Bailey just called me from prison."

His eyes widened. "What the hell did he want?"

"He says he has information on the cases."

"Which cases?"

"He knows someone is copying my previous cases. He says the person who's doing it has been writing to him in prison and he wants to talk to me about it."

Shawn's lips thinned. "I don't like it. He's playing with you."

"I don't like it either, but what choice have I got?" She fixed her gaze on him. "He *knew*, Shawn. That thing I've been wondering about all this time, that I was the thing that connected those three cases, I just had the man who murdered my husband confirm it to me. And he says there's going to be another one, and that he has information that might stop him."

"You still need to refuse to go."

She shook her head. "We've got nowhere on these cases, not even a lead. Whoever did this is laughing at us."

"So, you think the cases are all linked now?"

"Don't you?"

"There's no physical proof linking them."

"Maybe these letters will be what we need for that proof."

"And if they're not?"

"Then I haven't lost anything."

Shawn pursed his lips and stared at her.

"Stop looking at me like that," she said. "I can handle it."

"You can handle sitting across a table from the man who murdered your husband?"

Did he think she'd use this as an excuse to get in front of Bailey? What would she even be able to do to him? It wasn't as though she'd be able to sneak a weapon inside the prison, she'd be well searched before she got inside. She wouldn't be able to get much more than a pen in there—not that she had any intention of stabbing Bailey with a pen. For one, prison officers would be nearby, plus it would take a well-aimed pen to kill a man. She wouldn't kill Bailey and she'd end up behind bars herself. She had no intention of making Poppy grow up without her mother as well as her father, or sacrificing her job and the relationships she had with her colleagues. Her love for those things was far greater than her hatred of Bailey.

"Yes, I can." She wasn't so sure how she'd react, but she wasn't going to let Shawn know that.

"What if he plans on hurting you?"

"How can he hurt me? He's in prison. He doesn't have any access to weapons, and I'll have one of the prison officers standing right outside the door.

"He's got his hands, his teeth. He can still cause you harm."

"The prison officers wouldn't allow it."

His nostrils flared. "Prison officers get hurt by inmates, too, Erica. There's no guarantee."

"Shawn, our job is dangerous. It comes with the territory. There will always be some risk, but I believe the payoff is worth it. What if Bailey can actually tell us something important and we catch whoever's been doing this? Or let me turn it around...what if I don't go, and he kills again? Which of my cases is he going to pick next? Will he rape and murder a teenage student perhaps? Or set off a bomb in the city?"

"We don't know for sure that's what's happening."

Erica's frustration burst from her, and she slammed her fist on the desk. "Nicholas Bailey knows! Why would he even think that unless it was true? I've just had my suspicions confirmed by the man I hate most in the world. How could that possibly happen unless it was the truth?"

"You're going to need to okay it with Gibbs."

"No, I'm not. He doesn't need to know about this. It doesn't directly link to any of the cases."

Shawn folded his arms across his chest. "In one breath you're saying that the cases must be connected because

Nicholas fucking Bailey says they are, and the next you're saying whatever Bailey knows might have nothing to do with the cases. Which is it?"

"I won't know that until after I've spoken to him. If it comes to anything, then I'll go to Gibbs."

Shawn shook his head. "You're kidding yourself, Erica. You're only telling yourself that because you know he won't like the idea either."

"He's overly cautious since the stroke. And there's no point in upsetting him about something that might amount to nothing. If Bailey is bullshitting me, Gibbs doesn't need to know."

"And if he's not?"

"Then we'll need to look into things in more detail and then of course I'll bring Gibbs up to speed."

Shawn exhaled a frustrated breath and ran his hand over the top of his head. "At least let me drive you there."

"Okay," she agreed. "But you need to wait in the car."

"Deal."

Chapter Twenty-Four

"**D**etective Inspector Erica Swift to see Nicholas Bailey."

Erica had managed to make an emergency appointment via legal visits. She passed through the scanner and did the same for her belongings, then showed her ID and Bailey's prisoner number to the prison reception. She waited while it was checked.

Nerves churned her stomach, and she didn't like it. She often thought about what she would say to Nicholas if she ever got to speak to him again, but she knew she would never say any of the things she'd imagined. They were all born from raw emotion, and she refused to give him access to that part of her. Any attempts to tap into his humanity, to make him see what he'd done to her and her daughter, would only be wasted breath. If anything, he'd probably revel in her pain. After all, that was the whole reason he'd murdered Chris in front of her. He'd wanted her to experience the same pain he had when his brother had died.

The grief she still felt from Chris's loss was a strange thing. There were times when she could go through her day, almost feeling like things were normal, but then something tiny would happen—something that reminded her of before—and it would hit her like a punch, flooring her. She'd often found herself lying in bed, unable to sleep and gasping with the sheer helpless pain of it. At night, with the long hours ahead of her until morning, and no way to distract her thoughts was always the hardest time. It was the time when she would go over every moment, every word spoken, each action, and question what she could have done differently. It was also then when she'd have those imaginary conversations with Nicolas Bailey, where she tore him to shreds with the vitriol of her words, and hurt him in such a way that he'd never have another peaceful moment in his life.

But expecting to impact him in such a way meant pretending that Nicholas thought and felt the same way as regular people. Someone who did what he'd done didn't give a thought to how his actions affected others. The only person Nicholas Bailey had ever cared about, other than his brother, was Nicholas Bailey.

The security officer handed her back her ID. "Wait here and one of the officers will walk you down."

"Thank you."

This wasn't the first time she'd had to interview a prisoner, but this was the first time she'd ever felt particularly anxious about it. She was normally so self-assured in her line of work. She knew she was on the right side of the law and she took confidence in that. Why did Bailey have contact with whoever was doing these killings, and why had he felt the need to contact her about it? Could it be that he'd grown a conscience over the past two years and regretted what he'd done to her family? Could this be his way of making it up to her? But why had the killer chosen to get in touch with Nicholas Bailey in the first place?

Legal visits didn't take place in the same visiting hall as the others, and instead had a dedicated room. A male prison officer arrived to take her there. He looked her up and down, his lip curling in what was supposed to have been a smile, but more resembled a sneer. Her gaze flicked to his name badge, Officer Bache.

"This way," he grunted, leading her down the corridor to the legal visits interview room.

The clangs of metal doors shutting, and the distant shouts of prisoners, filled her ears. It was hot in here, too, and sweat trickled from her nape and down her spine.

She swallowed hard and wiped her clammy palms on the sides of her trousers. She didn't want Bailey to notice how nervous she was. It was important she remained unaffected by his presence, no matter what he told her. She gave the officer a nod to say she was ready, and he reached past her and opened the door.

Erica stepped through.

"Hello, Nicholas."

Nicholas Bailey sat on the other side of the table. He looked exactly the same as she remembered. The two years in prison hadn't aged him at all. How old was he now? Mid-twenties? She felt sure she'd aged after everything that had happened. Losing her husband, dealing with her daughter's grief as well as her own, remaining at work the entire time, had certainly given her a few new grey hairs and some extra lines. Maybe she'd have had them anyway, even if she hadn't lost Chris. She was closer to forty now than she was thirty.

"Hello, Detective."

His tone was low and quiet, so she strained to hear. He didn't meet her eye.

She went to the chair and pulled it back but didn't sit yet. "I must admit, you're the last person I thought I would be visiting."

Erica slipped into the chair and placed a digital micro recorder on the table. "Do I have your consent to record our interview?"

"I suppose so."

She clicked the record button. "Interview conducted by DI Swift with Nicholas Bailey." She gave their location and time and date, and then laced her fingers together on top of the table.

His gaze flickered up to hers and then slid back down again. "I wasn't sure you'd even come."

"Why wouldn't I? It's my job to catch people like you, and if you have information on who's killing those people, I need to know about it. Tell me about the letters. When did you first start receiving them?"

He rolled his lips together, thinking. "A year ago. More. Maybe eighteen months."

Eighteen months ago? That wasn't long after Nicholas had first been put away. Could someone have been planning the murders all this time? That was one hell of a long game they were playing. The idea of that made her uncomfortable. Had someone been watching her all that time, studying her cases, and handpicking the ones they thought they could replicate? Had it started with Nicholas's case? It made sense that it had. It had been a high-profile case, and because of Chris's murder, it had been all over the newspapers and social media.

"And how many letters have you received since?"

"Not many. One every few months."

"Do you know who's writing them?"

"No. He signs his name as M Cimi, but I don't think that'll be his real name."

Erica jotted it down anyway. Even if it wasn't a real name, it would mean something, or be connected in some way. Every bit of information was an important lead to follow, no matter how small it seemed.

"Are you sure you don't know the person who wrote you these letters, Nicholas? Has he been in to visit you at all?"

"No, I don't know who he is. I've never met him before in my life."

"Do you still have those letters?"

"No, I don't." He glanced down at his hands.

She leaned forward slightly. "Are you sure about that, Nicholas?"

"I destroyed the letters. I knew someone would find them and use them against me."

"All of them?" She didn't believe him. Nicholas had been alone for so long, both inside the prison and when he'd been on the outside, too. He'd killed because he'd wanted people to take him seriously. Someone had considered him important enough to put pen to paper, so would Nicholas really have destroyed that?

She needed to get her hands on them, even if it was only one. There were things they could find from the letters, information in people's handwriting that could be analysed. Maybe even fingerprints from the paper, DNA from the saliva on the envelopes, hair, and clothing fibres.

She tried again. "Nicholas, if you'd destroyed all the letters, why would you bother to contact me? Surely you must realise that I'm not going to take you seriously unless you can offer me proof."

"It might have been a way of getting you in here."

She tried not to rise to it. "Is that the truth, because I don't believe you, Nicholas. You're saying someone has taken the time to write to you, and you destroyed their letters? If I get one of the prison officers to search your cell, are you really saying they won't find anything?"

His lips tightened. "They won't find anything."

"Then what am I doing here?"

"I'll give you one of the letters he's sent me, and I'll tell you everything else I know, but on one condition."

"Which is?"

"I want that reduced sentence. I want to get out of here before I hit old age. I want to still have a life."

She grew cold inside. "You don't deserve to have a life when you took life from so many others."

"Including your husband, isn't that right, Detective?"

Erica balled her hands into fists beneath the table. "Why did this person choose you to contact? Did you do something to encourage him?"

"No, I didn't. At least, nothing since I've been in here."

"You're saying he contacted you because of...of what you did before?"

He lifted his gaze and held eye contact properly for the first time. "Because of what I did to your husband."

A cold fist tightened around her heart. She wasn't a violent person, but in that moment, it took every ounce of self-control not to climb across the table and tear at his face with her nails. She felt all the blood drain from her cheeks.

"Don't you think it's more likely to be because of all the people you hurt before?" She was thinking of Brandon Skehan and the way this person might have tried to cut his eye out.

"Perhaps, but I don't believe so. He's been copying the cases you've worked on. My case is just one small part of the plan."

She remembered the way Naomi's murder had reminded her of the Maher case and the burned body of the second victim made her think of the black-market organ case. She was the one who'd led both investigations. Could Nicholas be right? Was she what was connecting the murders? It wasn't as though she hadn't considered the possibility herself.

"Did this person mention my name?" she dared to ask.

"Not in so many words."

She narrowed her eyes. "What does that mean?"

"He talked about birds."

Erica frowned. "Birds?"

He raised his chin. "Because of your surname."

Birds? That was an obscure connection to make. Was Bailey just reading something into this that wasn't there? Without seeing the letters for herself, it was impossible to tell.

Chapter Twenty-Five
Present Day

Detective Inspector Erica Swift was younger than he remembered, prettier, too. He had to keep reminding himself that she was the one who'd been there when his brother had died. She was the one who could have helped Danny and didn't. It was strange, but he felt distanced from those events now, as though it had happened to a different person. He hadn't expected to feel that way at all.

Now someone else was out there, wanting to kill her. Should he warn her? Tell her to watch her back?

"Don't you dare tell her."

Nicholas recognised the voice instantly, and his heart lurched into his throat.

He glanced over his shoulder to find his brother leaning against the wall, his arms folded over his chest. He looked exactly the same as the last time Nicholas had seen him.

Danny?

Danny had always been younger than him, but now the age difference was noticeable. Of course, Nicholas had continued to age, while Danny hadn't, because Danny was dead.

Danny hissed from behind his shoulder. "She doesn't deserve your help."

He had to warn her, didn't he? No, he didn't. He didn't have to warn her at all. Hadn't he wanted her punished?

But I have punished her. I took her husband.

Danny turned and slammed his hand down on the nearest table. Nicholas jumped, but no one else in the room seemed to hear the bang. The detective had noticed Nicholas's reaction, though, she'd seen him start, but didn't understand the reason behind it. He saw her curiosity, tinged with unease, as she stared at him, her pretty ocean-coloured eyes narrowed. She knew he'd heard something, but she didn't know what.

He resisted the urge to spin around and tell Danny to shut up. If he did that, they'd think he was insane, and they'd never take him seriously.

M Cimi was going to kill the detective. It would probably happen soon, long before Nicholas would get out of here and be able to do it himself. Nicholas should be happy, it should be what he wanted, but now she was sitting here with him, he was filled with a sense of unease. She was a mother. If she died, there would be another child who would grow up in the system. He'd taken away the child's father, and while he'd planned on taking Erica's eyes, he hadn't planned to kill her, had he? Cimi wanted her dead, though. Nicholas didn't know why, but he did.

Warn her. Tell her he's coming after her next.

The words buzzed inside him like wasps around a disturbed nest. He had an opportunity here to do something right for once in his life. He knew exactly what those letters meant. Hadn't he been the one to reach out to her in the first place? What had been his reason for doing that if he hadn't wanted to help? Was it just so he could insert himself back into her life again, to make sure he was remembered, and not left here languishing in this hellhole while she continued with her life?

"Are you still with us, Nicholas?"

DI Swift's cool tone broke through his thoughts, and he cleared his throat. "Yes, I'm still with you."

"Because you looked distracted. Something you've thought of that you'd like to tell me, perhaps?"

Tell her, tell her!

"Don't you dare tell her, Nicholas," Danny growled. "Let the bitch get what's coming to her."

Nicholas clenched his fists, and a strange whining came from deep within his throat. He squeezed his eyes shut, hoping that when he opened them again, Danny wouldn't be there. Could anyone else see him? No, of course they couldn't. Thinking such a thing was mad. But wasn't seeing your dead brother also crazy? He was sure he'd heard somewhere that people didn't consciously know when they were mad. It was a gradual thing that crept in slowly, convincing your mind that the insane things it was being shown were real. Nicholas knew that he shouldn't be seeing his dead brother in prison—even if he was alive, he wouldn't have been able to get in—yet here he was.

What did it mean? Was Danny really here, or was Nicholas crazy? There was no other possibility.

When he opened his eyes, his brother was still standing there, staring at him in a combination of disapproval and disappointment.

"I'm not going to just vanish, Nicholas," Danny said. "I'm here to help you."

"Nicholas?" Erica asked again, her eyebrows raised.

"It's nothing. I don't have anything more to tell you."

"That's not true, is it? You called me directly because you're receiving letters and you believe they're linked to some of my investigations. But you've been receiving these letters for months, so why suddenly call me now? What did the letter say that prompted that call?"

That she's next.

"Keep your mouth shut," Danny hissed. "I mean it."

His brother couldn't control him anymore. Danny was dead, and he'd been dead for years. Nicholas knew this, but still the Danny standing behind him felt as real as he ever had. Nicholas had always been frightened by what his brother was capable of. Danny had buried their mother's body without barely batting an eyelid, while Nicholas had hidden in his room with his hands over his head, rocking in the corner. They might not have been the one to kill her, but Nicholas sometimes wondered if Danny would have killed her anyway, if she hadn't died on her own. It had affected Danny, though, even if he'd acted as though he hadn't given a shit. The drinking had started, and his temper had got worse. And look how things had ended for him.

For both of them.

DI Swift could have changed things for them, and she hadn't. If Danny had lived that day, maybe Nicholas's life would have gone down a different route, too.

"Nicholas?" The detective's voice again. "Are you all right?"

Nicholas forced himself to straighten in his chair. "I'm done here. Come back with a signed agreement that gets me a reduced sentence and we'll talk again."

"It's not a decision I can make. I don't have the authority. I'd need to take it higher up the chain and put the request in to a senior detective."

He sat back in his chair and folded his arms. "What are you waiting for?" He raised his voice. "Officer. I'm done."

He clamped his lips shut, determined not to say another word.

The door opened, and Officer Bache stepped in. His line of sight was on DI Swift instead of Nicholas, but Nicholas knew Bache would take any opportunity to get him in trouble again.

"Everything okay in here, Detective?"

DI Swift nodded to the officer and spoke the time of the end of the interview into the recorder before switching it off and getting to her feet. "Looks like we're finished."

Chapter Twenty-Six

Nicholas Bailey was hiding something. She couldn't say for certain what it was, but he was on edge and wired. There was little doubt in her mind that Nicholas suffered from mental health issues—what kind of person would do the things he had in the past if they were mentally well?—but this felt different. It was almost as though there were more people in the room than just the two of them and the prison officer outside the door.

Erica stepped into the corridor outside the room and turned to the officer. "Can you take me to see Governor Hughes?"

"He might be busy."

"Well, he's going to have to make time."

Officer Bache rolled his eyes, but he jerked his head down the corridor. "This way."

She followed him down until they reached an office door with 'Governor Nigel Hughes' on it.

The prison officer knocked and then entered. She heard him explain who she was and what she was doing there to the governor. Then he stepped out again and nodded for her to go in.

Erica entered to find an overweight man in his sixties sitting behind a desk.

"DI Swift," he said, not getting up to greet her. "What can I do for you?"

"I'm going to need Nicholas Bailey's cell turned. He says he's been receiving letters from the suspect in a case I've been investigating, but that he's destroyed them, but in the next breath he says he's got a letter he can give me. He must have it somewhere."

The governor shrugged. "It wouldn't be unusual for a prisoner to destroy mail, especially if it contained something they didn't want other people to see."

"Like what? Surely the letters are checked before they're handed over to the prisoners?"

"They are, but not in detail. We have almost a thousand prisoners here. It would be impossible to read everything word for word, and of course we're not allowed to check anything that's of a legal matter."

"These letters weren't of a legal matter. They were letters from a killer to a killer."

Governor Hughes linked his fingers together. "Okay, we can get that done."

"There's one more thing," she said. "I don't want Bailey to know that we've gone through his cell."

"Why not?"

"I want him to think he's got the upper hand, at least for the moment. Watch his incoming mail, though. Anything that's addressed to him needs to be treated as evidence in a case. I want it bagged up and for you to call me immediately."

"Okay, we can do that."

"Thank you."

"Prisoners get an hour of outdoor exercise each day. We could search the cell then."

"You'd need to take photographs before you search it, make sure everything is put back just as it is. If you find any letters, take photographs, and then put them back again."

Ideally, she'd like to take any letters and have them forensically analysed, but doing so would mean no more information from Nicholas. He'd clam up on them. If there were things in the letters that he had destroyed that might prove important, they would only know about it if Nicholas told them. He wouldn't do that if he thought he could no longer trust her.

It was a gamble, though. Perhaps she'd be better with the letters than Nicholas's confidence. If they got a fingerprint from it that matched one on file, they'd be able to pin down their suspect.

Was she making a mistake?

Internally, she warred with herself. If Nicholas saw they'd betrayed his trust, he might even find a way to warn the person he was in contact with. They might lose this lead for good.

Chapter Twenty-Seven

Erica sucked in a breath to calm her nerves and knocked on her boss's door.

"Yes?" he called out from inside.

Erica opened the door and entered. "Sorry to disturb you, sir, but there's something I need to talk to you about."

He frowned and put down his pen. "That sounds serious."

"It is."

Gibbs gestured to the chair on the other side of his desk as an indication for her to sit. She did so.

He put his elbows on the desk and steepled his fingers to his lips. "So, what is it you need to talk to me about?"

"I went to the prison today…to speak to Nicholas Bailey."

Gibbs sat up straighter. "What? Why?"

"He phoned me and asked me to come in and see him. He believes he has information on the cases I've been working on, and one of DI Carlton's cases. I had my suspicions that they were all connected, and Nicholas Bailey has confirmed it for me."

"How could they possibly be connected?"

"Through me. Someone is copying my past cases. Someone tried to cut Brandon's Skehan's eye out, and before that, he must have strangled Naomi Conrad in her bed, though her body wasn't discovered until after the attack on Brandon Skehan. Then the same person burned a body down on the canal path on the Isle of Dogs."

"And you can be certain the same person is responsible for all three? Do you have forensics linking the three crimes?"

Erica twisted her hands together in her lap. "No, sir. I don't."

"So how can you be sure?"

"Because the person responsible has been writing to Nicholas Bailey about the crimes."

Gibbs frowned. "Shouldn't that have been picked up by the prison staff when they were checking the incoming post?"

"The letters were written in a way that it wasn't obvious."

"Then how can you be certain?"

"Because he *knew*, sir. He confirmed what I was already thinking. How could he have possibly made the connection otherwise?"

"The news?"

She shook her head. "No, I believe him."

Gibbs huffed out a breath of frustration. "You should have sent someone else. You're too emotionally involved with Nicholas Bailey."

"I couldn't. I was the only person he would speak to."

He rubbed his fingers over his lips. There was still a shadow that hung about him from the stroke—not a shadow, a ghost. A slight weakness to the side that had been most badly affected, a droop to his eyelid and the way that side of his mouth didn't lift properly when he smiled. Luckily for Gibbs, smiling wasn't something he did too often anyway.

"I understand that. I just worry about you, Swift. It's all a bit much, after everything you've been through."

"Thank you, sir, but I'm strong. I've had to be. And if this helps catch whoever is playing games with us, then I'll do whatever it takes."

"I know you are. Don't push yourself to do anything that's going to be damaging to you, or put yourself in a situation where you think there's the chance of you losing control. This isn't worth losing you as a detective."

"I won't do anything stupid, sir."

Did he think she'd hurt Bailey? Maybe it was an understandable concern. Hadn't she thought about it often enough? In the early days, when she'd been consumed by rage and grief, she'd pictured herself wrapping her hands around Bailey's throat and squeezing and squeezing and squeezing. She'd wanted to punch and kick and claw, and make him feel every drop of pain that she had.

Now she had some distance, and while she would never forgive Bailey for what he'd done to their family, she no longer felt consumed by her emotions. Her main focus was catching whoever had killed Naomi and attacked Brandon and set fire to the as yet unnamed body by the canal. They would do it again, she was sure. Which of her past cases would he choose from next? There had been plenty over the course of her career.

She couldn't do anything to bring Chris back, but she could prevent more people being killed, and that was what she needed to focus on.

"You don't need to worry about me, sir. I promise."

He exhaled a long breath. "I do worry, and that's not going to change, but I do trust that you know yourself well enough to understand your own motivations."

"My only motivation is finding our suspect."

His lips twitched, and she realised he'd tried to smile.

"That's what I thought."

"I have the prison guards searching his cell for the letters, but I haven't heard from them yet. But Bailey says he'll let us have one of the letters he's kept—one that'll tell us who's next on this psychopath's list—and help us catch him. Of course, that doesn't come without a caveat attached to it."

"Which is?"

"He wants a reduced sentence."

"Not going to happen."

"Then someone else is going to die. We have nothing, sir. No leads at all. This could finally give us something to catch that son of a bitch."

Gibbs thought for a moment. "This is something I'm going to have to take higher up the food chain," he said. "It's not a decision I can make alone."

"But you will support it," she pressed.

He fixed her in place through eye contact alone. "You really want to help the man who murdered your husband get out of prison early?"

She made sure she wasn't the first to break it. "If it means saving lives and putting another murderer behind bars, then yes, sir. I do."

Chapter Twenty-Eight

Abi Kebell had been working at the prison for almost five years now. Her friends thought it was a strange career for a woman to want to follow, but Abi couldn't understand what the problem was. It was a steady job that paid the bills, and she enjoyed it. Her friends imagined she spent the day getting spat at and suffering abuse from the prisoners, but it wasn't like that at all. Of course, there were days when that happened, but that was normally when someone new was brought in and they were still raging against the world. She didn't get it any worse than her male counterparts.

Anyway, some of her fellow officers were worse than the prisoners. She'd overheard Officer Bache say more than once that the only good prisoner was a dead prisoner. Sure, she got the odd catcall or suggestive comment, but it was no worse than she'd experience on a night out in town. After she got to know the prisoners—especially the long-timers –she found they were perfectly respectful towards her.

Nicholas Bailey sat alone at one of the eight tables that were positioned at equal distances from each other in a rectangle in the middle of the library. He huddled over a book in the same way a school student might hunch over a paper during a test, suspicious and protective.

She'd heard about what Bailey had done to get himself put inside here in the first place. If she hadn't already known, she would never have thought him capable of such a horrific thing. He was tall and lanky, and walked with his shoulders hunched and head down. He barely made eye contact with anyone, and had a shy but polite way of speaking when he was spoken to. She couldn't imagine him with a knife in his hand, gouging out peoples' eyes. And he'd pushed a police officer's husband under a Tube train, too.

A shudder crept its way over her shoulders and she gave herself a shake. It wasn't like her to get unsettled by someone. She wasn't the type of person to be easily spooked. She'd happily watch a horror film on her own and then go up to bed in the dark.

Bailey looked up from his book, and for a moment she thought he was going to look directly at her. But instead, he glanced over his shoulder and muttered something unintelligible. His head tilted to one side, as though he was listening to a reply, and then he shook his head and went back to his book.

Abi froze. Who was he talking to? Her line of sight skittered to the point Bailey had been focused on. She half expected to find someone standing there that she hadn't noticed before, but the space was empty. There were a number of other prisoners milling around the library, either sitting at one of the other tables or browsing the shelves. Plenty of the inmates took this time inside to further their educations. The other inmates interacted with each other, however. Even if one of them was sitting down, they might get a friendly punch on the shoulder from someone else, or another prisoner might join them on the same table, or talk to them while they were checking out books on the shelves. Occasionally, they got too loud, and Abi would find herself having to shush them like a regular librarian. They were generally pretty good about her telling them off, even if they might throw the odd comment to raise a chuckle from their peers.

Bailey turned his head again and said something under his breath.

Abi noted how none of the other prisoners engaged with him either. They all gave him a wide berth, as though even in this confined space where they were all criminals, they still sensed he was something different.

One of the other inmates wanted to check out a book, distracting her for a moment. When she looked back, Bailey was no longer at the table, and the book he'd been reading was gone, too. Where was he? Why didn't he check out the book to read in his cell if it was on a topic he clearly found to be interesting?

She rose from her desk, but movement by one of the bookcases made her stop. Bailey emerged from between the shelves, and she sank back down into her seat. Once this group's time was up, she'd go and check what Bailey was reading.

The prisoners were taken back to their cells, and Abi had a little time before the next group arrived. She got to her feet and slipped down between the shelves, making her way to the rear of the library where Bailey had put the book back on the right shelf, together with the others in its genre. She remembered the one she'd pointed him towards. He picked the same one out every time he came back.

She trailed her fingertips across the spines and paused at the correct book. She tweaked it out from between its neighbours, weighed it in her grip, and then positioned the book so she could look at the cover.

The Complete Guide to British Birds.

She remembered him asking her about it a couple of months earlier. Why was he still reading the same book? She opened it and flipped through the pages. Something inside the paper slip of the hardcover. Folded and wedged into the corner. Abi frowned and picked it out. She unfolded the piece of paper and stared down at it.

A letter. Addressed to Nicholas Bailey.

Hadn't there been a detective in, asking about letters? She was sure some of the other officers had been talking about it.

Her heart suddenly slammed against the inside of her ribs. Was this what the police had been searching for? They'd done a search of his cell during his exercise hour, and despite pulling the place apart, hadn't found anything that had given them cause for concern.

She realised she was touching it with her fingers.

"Shit." She knew enough about forensics to understand that she'd be contaminating any DNA or fingerprints the police might be able to get from the paper. It probably wouldn't be easy, since now not only had she handled it, but Bailey had, too, and most likely it had also been handled by whichever prison officer had been checking the incoming post the day it had arrived. It had also been moved around, ending up secured in the cover of this book, so it wasn't as though it had been kept in an evidence bag for protection either.

She kept hold of the book. She'd take it down to Governor Hughes, and he could call the detective who'd been interested in Bailey.

Abi left the library, the book clutched in her hands, and almost ran into one of her colleagues.

"What have you got there, Kebell?" Prison Officer Bache asked her.

She answered his question with one of her own. "What was the name of that detective who was here the other day, speaking to Nicholas Bailey?"

His eyes narrowed. "Why do you want to know that?"

She didn't trust Bache with the truth. "He mentioned something to me in the library just now. I want to run it by her."

"What did he say?"

"It's probably nothing, but like I said, I want to run it by her."

He took a step forwards, putting his shoulders back and blowing out his chest like a cartoon character. "How about you run it by me first?"

She fought to remained unperturbed. Considering the kinds of men she had to deal with every single day, she wasn't going to let a colleague try to intimidate her. Men like Ian Bache were simple bullies who relied on their size and physical strength to get their own way.

"Why would I want to do that? You're not my boss."

"No, but I'm a colleague who has plenty more experience than you, and not to mention respect."

She had to stop herself snorting at that. The only person who respected Bache was himself. Even the prisoners thought he was a dickhead. She was surprised one of them hadn't turned on him already. She'd heard plenty of rumours about how he liked to bait some of the smaller, weaker prisoners, winding them up about the things they cared about, such as their families on the outside. He'd see a photograph of a wife or girlfriend stuck to a cell wall, and either call the woman names like fat pig or say she had a face only a mother could love, or if she was attractive, would tell the prisoner how she was most likely out shagging her way around the rest of the city by now. If the prisoner had children, that was an even easier way to wind them up, talking about how the kids wouldn't even know who Daddy was by the time they got out, and how another man would soon take their place in their children's hearts. Bache poked and poked at them until they eventually retaliated, and then they'd be the ones in trouble for assaulting one of the prison officers, and they'd find themselves at an adjudication where, if found guilty, their punishment might be anything from loss of canteen rights to solitary confinement, or even days added to their sentence.

"Don't worry, I'll go and ask the governor." She shrugged and moved to get past him. "I'll let him know you refused to help me."

She hadn't taken part in the turn down, but Bache had.

"Fine. Her name is Swift. DI Swift. She's one of these bitches who thinks she's something special just because of her job. Bossing everyone around like she owned the place."

Bache thought every woman was a bitch. He probably even thought of his own mother that way.

"Thanks for your help, Bache. Always a pleasure talking to you."

Chapter Twenty-Nine

Erica answered her phone. "DI Swift." She didn't recognise the number calling.

"It's Governor Hughes here, from the prison."

"Of course. What can I do for you?"

"We have something you've been looking for."

"You found the letters?" she guessed. "I thought you didn't find anything in his cell."

"We didn't. Let me hand you over to one of our prison officers and she can explain in more detail."

A female voice replaced the governor's gruff, deep one. "My name is Abi Kebell, and I work in the prison library. I believe I've found one of the letters belonging to Nicholas Bailey that you've been looking for. I'm not sure what he's done with the others, though, you might want to do a thorough search of the library now."

"The library?"

"Yes, that's where I found the letter. It was hidden inside a book he likes to read. He spends whatever time he can up here. I thought he was interested in the subject he was reading, but now I'm wondering if he was just reading the letter the whole time."

"What's the subject of the book?"

"British bird life," Abi said.

Erica remembered what Nicholas had said about the letter talking about birds and how he'd made that connection to her surname.

"And what have you done with the letter?"

"I'm sorry, but I touched it initially, before I realised what I had. I've got it in a plastic bag now."

"That's perfect. Can you pass me back to Governor Hughes now, please?"

"Yes, of course."

There was a slight scuffle as the phone was handed over, and then Governor Hughes came back on the line.

"I'm going to send a Scenes of Crime officer down to you to collect the letter, and I'll meet them down there. I need you to make sure no one else goes into the library. We're going to need the place thoroughly searched."

"The prisoners aren't going to appreciate losing their library time."

"I'm afraid there isn't much I can do about that. In the meantime, I suggest you keep Bailey in his cell. We don't want him getting wind of this and destroying any remaining letters."

"That I can do."

Erica hung up and immediately started a new call to get SOCO down to the prison, then she went to update Gibbs.

"Could this be a breakthrough?" he asked.

"I'm hoping so. It'll depend on what forensics can get from the letter. Have you heard anything about a deal to reduce Bailey's sentence yet?"

"Not yet, but if we can get what we need from the letter, we might not need to go down that route."

She hoped he was right.

She left Gibbs's office, and Shawn stopped her on the way to her desk.

"Did you hear?" she asked him. "One of the prison officers has found one of the letters Bailey received. I've got SOCO going down there now, but I want to get a look at it. You want to come?"

He grabbed his jacket. "Count me in."

• • • •

THE GOVERNOR WAS ALREADY there to meet them, as was Lee Mattocks, head of Scenes of Crime for their borough. Lee was a tall, lanky man, and Erica had never seen him in anything other than a charcoal-grey suit. Either he owned several identical suits, or he just wore the same thing every day.

Lee had already taken possession of the letter and was taking photographs of it to upload.

"We need to do a search on the prison library," she told him. "There might be more letters hidden in the books."

She took the plastic bag containing the piece of paper. There was nothing about the letter that gave them any clues—no heading or address on it.

She glanced at the name signed at the bottom. *M Cimi.* If it wasn't the killer's real name, what did it mean?

"This one must be talking about the Maher case," Erica said, reading through it. "I can see why it got past the staff checking the post. Unless you knew the backstory to the cases, it would seem completely innocent."

She kept reading, holding it out so Shawn could see it, too. The words sent chills down her spine.

'...there is something about the scent of oil paints and solvent in the air that makes me feel alive. It means something to create, to take a blank canvas and transform it into a piece of art that has meaning. I even enjoy scrubbing the paint from my hands

afterwards, the way the red paint swirls against the white porcelain of the sink.'

Shawn frowned. "Why do I feel as though I've read this before?"

Erica looked up at him. "What do you mean?"

"I'm not sure, but I feel like I'm getting a case of déjà vu." He turned his head, gazing into the distance, lines appearing between his brows as he thought. Suddenly, he snapped his fingers. "I've got it. The letters that Lara Maher gave you. I read through them in more detail. They're not all hate mail. One of them asks Lara to forward their letter to Tristan. It talks about a shared interest in art, as though that psychopath didn't murder his victims before he painted them."

Erica gaped at him. "Did you send those letters off to forensics, like you said?"

"Yes, I did, but I told them there was no rush on it."

"Does the handwriting appear to be the same?" she asked.

He stared at the letter. "Honestly, it's hard to tell, but the turn of phrase and the tone used was very similar."

"So, the same person who wrote to Nicholas Bailey about the murders also wrote to Lara Maher." Erica couldn't believe it. They'd had evidence this whole time and didn't know it. "Do we have a date on the letter Lara received?"

"No, but I believe she put them in chronological order, as and when she received them. That one had been at the back of the pile, so she must have been sent it not long after her brother was caught."

"Could it be that the killer was already planning to copy these murders even then? First Nicholas Bailey and then Tristan Maher."

"And more recently," Shawn said, "the black-market organ case."

"Shit. So, what might be next?" Her mind was spinning, trying to think of the multitude of cases she'd covered over the past couple of years.

In what order had the murders happened? Did they correlate to the order of her previous cases? If so, perhaps she could use them to figure out which one was next? But no, even though Brandon's attack had been reported first, Naomi's murder had actually happened earlier, so that put any theory that the killer was doing them in a particular order down the drain.

"He's not following the same order as the cases," she said. "There has to be something else."

"Without all of the letters, it's hard to tell. Let's hope the search on the library uncovers the others."

Erica blew out a breath. "Should we talk to Bailey again? If he knows we're going to find the letters without him, he might feel he's got no choice but to talk."

Shawn shook his head. "I doubt he will. He's lost his upper hand. What will he gain by talking to us?"

"Even so, we should try."

"Not you," Shawn said firmly. "Let someone else go in this time. You're too emotionally involved with this."

For once, she relented. She told herself it was because she'd be better off chasing forensics about the letter sent to Lara Maher, but perhaps, deep down, she knew Shawn was right. She was too emotionally involved, and besides, she highly doubted Nicholas would tell them anything now.

Erica brought DI Carlton up to speed about what they'd learned. The body burned down by the canal was his case, and he needed to be informed about a possible suspect, even if they didn't have the real name of that person yet. "I'll come down to the prison," he said, "oversee things for a while, if you've got other things you need to be doing?"

"That would be great, thanks."

Shawn was going to talk to Bailey, while SOCO worked on the library. Going through each book meticulously was going to take time. With the possible link between the letters she'd taken from Lara Maher and the one they'd found, she headed back into the office to make sure forensics put a rush on them. She wished she'd photographed each one before handing them over, but at the time it hadn't seemed important.

Her phone buzzed, and she glanced at the screen. A text message from Brandon Skehan. *Can you come round? I've found something important. I think it might be evidence from my attack.*

She frowned and messaged back. *Come down to the station. We can talk about it there.*

Within seconds, the reply came back. *Can't. Think I'm suffering from a spot of agoraphobia since the attack. Haven't been able to leave the flat.*

Shit. She chewed her lip, thinking.

"Everything okay, boss?" DC Rudd asked her.

"Yes, fine. Brandon Skehan thinks he's found something important that might help us with the case. I need to pick up

Poppy soon, but I'm going to swing around there first. Can you let me know the moment forensics comes back with a report on the Maher letters?"

"Yes, of course."

Erica left the office and drove over to Skehan's flat and parked outside.

He opened the door as soon as she knocked, as though he was literally waiting at the door for her. He still had the white bandage covering the part of his face where he'd been cut. She couldn't help looking at it differently now. Had the same person who'd cut Brandon also murdered Naomi and set fire to the body down by the canal? They'd also been writing letters for months, if not years before then. Brandon was a small piece in a much more complex puzzle.

"Thank you for coming so fast."

He stepped aside to allow her in and then closed the door behind her.

"Not at all. How are you?"

"I've been better. You probably think I'm a complete idiot, don't you? I mean, the attack happened in this flat, so really it should be the last place I'd want to be."

He flashed her that winning smile, only this time it was awkward and a little unsure of itself.

"There's no right or wrong way to process something like this. Everyone reacts differently. Sometimes a victim can internalise the trauma and it'll be weeks or months until it makes itself known."

He bit on his lower lip, and his gaze darted down. "I don't like to think of myself as a victim."

"No, I understand that."

She did understand. Being a victim brought with it a stigma. It made you feel weak and helpless, and others treated you differently.

He motioned for her to go through to the kitchen. "I made us some tea. I hope that's okay. It's probably another stupid thing I've done, but I haven't seen or spoken to another person in days."

"Oh, right. I don't really have time for tea, sorry."

But he was already scooping teabags out of the mugs and adding in milk. He gestured for her to sit, and so she slid into one of the chairs at the kitchen table and he placed one of the mugs in front of her.

"When you messaged me," she said, "you mentioned you'd found something important? Some evidence from the attack?"

She lifted the mug and took a sip of the still hot tea. Between rushing around from the office to the prison and back again, she couldn't remember the last time she'd had anything to eat or drink, and she discovered she was in need of the pick-me-up.

"Yes, of course. That's why you're here. I know it's not a social call."

He reached for the kitchen worktop and picked up a plastic freezer bag with something inside it. He slid it onto the table in front of her.

Erica stared down at it. The bag contained a glove, the clear, thin kind used in medical practises. It was bundled into a ball, but the dark streaks were clearly visible.

She pulled her own gloves from her jacket pocket—she always kept them on her person, just in case—and snapped them on. She lifted the bag up to eye level and frowned. Were those dark spots dried blood droplets? If so, was it Brandon's blood? Whoever had attacked him must have been wearing gloves, since there were no prints on the handle of the knife. Could she hope that this was the glove he wore? If so, with any luck, forensics would be able to get DNA from the inside of it. If they could match it to a sample they already had on file, she might not just be able to catch whoever had attacked Brandon, but also whoever had murdered Naomi, and the person who set fire to the unidentified body down by the canal.

The same person who'd been writing to Nicholas Bailey in prison.

"Where did you find it?" Erica asked him.

"In the back garden, stuffed down between the wall and the shed."

"How on earth could our forensics team have missed that?"

"Honestly, I don't know. I guess someone wasn't doing their job properly."

A prickle of unease went through her. Something didn't ring true. "I've worked with that team on multiple occasions before and they've never given me any reason to think they aren't one hundred percent focused on their jobs. For them to have missed something as large as a discarded glove would have been a massive oversight."

This was the sort of mistake that could launch an internal enquiry.

"It's not always easy to get DNA from the inside of a vinyl glove, but we might get lucky."

The glove was turned inside out, which was normal when someone removed a close-fitting glove like this one. The person wearing it would have pulled it from the top, around the wrist rather than from the tips of the fingers, so causing it to turn inside out as it was removed. Then it had been left, exposed to the elements for several days, which again made it harder to get any DNA samples that would be of any use. That didn't mean it wasn't possible, though.

"You think it might help you find whoever did this?" Brandon asked.

"It's the most solid lead we've got," she admitted.

"I'll feel better once I know whoever did this is behind bars."

Erica lifted her mug and took a gulp of the tea. It had cooled enough now to drink.

"I'm going to need to get my team back here. If they missed this, there's a chance they missed something else important, too." She reached into her jacket pocket for her phone and pulled it out. Her mind was still reeling from the idea that they'd missed something as big as a glove.

"You don't want to do that, DI Swift."

His tone had changed, grown harder, and she looked up in surprise. "I'm sorry, what?"

"I only used the glove as a way of getting you here. No one missed it. I was wearing it the day of the attack."

Strangely, her head grew foggy, and the room seemed to tilt to one side. "What are you talking about?"

"Come on, you're the detective. You figure it out."

"*You* were wearing the glove? You did that to yourself?"

Her instinct was to rationalise this, but a wave of information flooded over her. The lack of fibres from the wall behind the house, where the attacker must have made his escape. That the dog hadn't barked when someone should have been scrambling over the wall and into the animal's garden. That the security footage from a few doors down had never caught anyone, and there hadn't been any sign of footprints either.

She'd thought at the time that it was as though the attacker had vanished into thin air, but what if the reason he'd disappeared so easily was that he never existed?

Had Brandon Skehan done this to himself?

A cold chill ran up Erica's spine and crept up over her shoulders like a pair of ghostly hands. Her skin rose in goosebumps, and she had to stop herself shuddering. What did this mean?

It was certainty that was solidifying inside her now. Brandon had cut his own face and lied to them about being attacked. And if he'd lied about that, what else hadn't he told her?

If each of the cases were connected, but Brandon was the assailant in his case, did that mean he was the assailant in the others as well? Was he the one who'd been writing to Nicholas Bailey in prison?

Brandon Skehan was M Cimi.

Erica got to her feet, but the room was wobbly around her. She glanced down at the tea. Shit. She should have known better than to accept a drink, but she'd grown to trust him. Her phone was in her hand. She needed to call Shawn and tell him what Brandon had done. She needed to ask for help. But her fingers didn't want to comply, and when she tried to swipe the screen to bring up Shawn's number, the phone clattered from her fingers and landed on the floor.

Chapter Thirty-One

Shawn knocked on the office door and entered before he got an answer. There was too much at risk here to waste even a single second. "Sir, we have a problem."

DCI Gibbs looked up from his paperwork. He appeared tired, but that might have simply been the effect of the way one side of his face still pulled down slightly on one side. If Shawn hadn't known what had happened, he might have just thought it was Gibbs's expression rather than the result of the stroke.

"Did Nicholas Bailey tell you something?"

Shawn shook his head. "No, he refused to speak, so I figured my time was better spent here."

"So, what's the problem?"

"Lara Maher, the sister of Tristan Maher, gave DI Swift a letter she received not long after her brother was put away. The letter has a distinct tone to it, very similar to what's been written to Nicholas Bailey in prison."

Gibbs steepled his fingers. "You think the letters were written by the same person?"

"I do, but that's not why I'm here. Forensics were able to get DNA from the letter that was written to Maher. It seems the care that was taken to make sure no DNA or fingerprints were on the letter written to Bailey wasn't given the same treatment as the one sent to Maher. Perhaps they hadn't known what they were going to do at that point so weren't worried about DNA, or perhaps they simply never thought the connection would be made between the two letters. Anyway, the point is that we've had a match."

"Who with?"

"Brandon Skehan."

Gibbs's lips pinched together, though one side still had some slackness. "Brandon Skehan? The man who was attacked in his home with a knife?"

"The same one. We took a DNA sample to cross-reference it against any samples taken from his flat, so we had it on file. He's the letter-writer, and DI Swift believes whoever is writing the letters is also the one who killed Naomi Conrad and the Jane Doe who was found by the canal. She thinks the killer is copying her old cases."

"Where is she now?"

"That's the problem. I'm not sure. She's not answering her phone."

Gibbs got to his feet. "Ask the others. Someone must know where she is."

DC Howard and Rudd were standing by Rudd's desk, looking over something. They both glanced up as Shawn strode over.

"Where's Swift?" he demanded.

Hannah Rudd straightened, concern marking her features as she took in his stance. "She's headed home. She needed to pick up her daughter, but I think she's swinging by one of the victim's homes on the way. He messaged her as she was leaving."

His blood ran cold. "One of the victims? Which victim?"

"Brandon Skehan. He said he'd remembered something that might help the case."

"Shit." He snatched his phone out of his pocket and swiped the screen to bring up her number. She was right at the top of his call list—he phoned her more than anyone else in his life.

He hit the 'call' button and placed the phone to his ear. *Pick up, Erica, damn it.* The phone rang a couple of times, and then the answerphone cut in, as though someone had deliberately refused the call.

"What's wrong?" DC Howard asked.

"We need to get there, now. Put a call out and get whichever patrol car is closest to his address to respond. Brandon Skehan isn't what he makes out to be. I think he cut his face himself and might be responsible for Naomi Conrad's murder, and the body discovered down by the canal as well."

"Did we ever ask him where he was the night Naomi Conrad was killed?" Rudd said.

"No, we didn't even make a connection between the two, at least Erica did, but not in the way she thought. She thought he was the victim of a copycat—someone who was copying her previous cases and writing to Nicholas Bailey about them—but she never suspected Skehan."

Gibbs marched over and must have seen all the worried faces. "She's still not answering her phone?"

Shawn shook his head. "No, she's not."

"That doesn't mean anything. She might just be driving," Rudd offered hopefully.

Shawn bit his lower lip. "I wish I could believe that, but my gut is telling me something else."

"Have we got Skehan's address?" Gibbs asked.

Shawn pulled it up from their records. "Yep, got it."

"Let's get over there, then," Gibbs said. "When we find him, I want him brought in for questioning. I want to know exactly where he was the night Naomi Conrad was killed."

"Wasn't he in hospital while all that was happening?" Rudd said.

Shawn shook his head. "No, think about it. Naomi was murdered before the 'attack' on him, but she wasn't found until a few days later. He did post videos to her social media via her phone to make it look as though she was still alive. Then the second body wasn't discovered until *after* he'd been released from hospital."

"Shit. So, is he M Cimi?" Rudd suddenly grabbed a pen and a piece of paper. "Look at what happens to the name if I move it around a little. Cimi back to front is imic. Add the 'M' and what do we have?"

"Mimic," Shawn finished for her. "And we need to find him. Now."

· · · ·

THEY PULLED UP AT SKEHAN'S house in a couple of unmarked cars. Two squad cars with their lights flashing had just pulled up to the address as well. If there was one thing that drew them all together, it was one of their own potentially in trouble. A BOLO had been issued for both Erica and Brandon Skehan, and they needed as many bodies on this as they could get.

Shawn jumped out of the pool car and raced up to the building. The shared door that led into the property was already open, and he stepped through the small entrance hall and hammered on the door to the flat. "Brandon Skehan. Open up. It's the police."

"DI Swift, are you in there?"

Her car is parked over there," Rudd said. "She's not in it."

"Get inside, now," Gibbs commanded.

Shawn lifted his leg and did a donkey kick, his shoe slamming against the wood, sending reverberations up his leg. Once, twice.

They had uniformed officers blocking the road behind, preventing Brandon from running.

The doorframe finally loosened—he was lucky it was old and hadn't been maintained. The frame cracked, and the inside of the lock was visible—a sliver of metal in the wood. He aimed another hard kick at the spot above the lock, and the door burst open.

"Skehan!" he yelled, careful not to rush in just in case Skehan was armed or might be in a position to hurt Erica. "The building is surrounded."

He took another couple of steps into the flat.

"Erica, are you in there?" He waited for a reply, but none came.

DC Howard jerked his chin in a silent question, asking if they should enter. Shawn nodded in return and led the way, stepping inside the property but keeping his back to the wall to protect himself. Gibbs remained outside, his physical condition meaning he was better off not getting into any potential tussles.

The flat wasn't big by any standard, and a matter of a few strides brought him to the doorway that led into the lounge. Quickly, he checked the room, DC Howard covering his back, while DC Rudd blocked the exit.

Empty.

He stepped back out and nodded farther down the hall. The next door led to a bedroom, which was also empty. He kept going to the back of the flat, where the kitchen and the back door leading onto the small garden was located. The kitchen was cramped and cluttered, with a wooden table and chairs at its centre. Two half-drunk cups of tea sat on the surface.

There was no sign of Erica, but he spotted something else. "What is that?"

He snapped on a glove from his pocket and picked up the bag, the plastic dangling between his thumb and forefinger. Inside was a balled-up glove, similar to the one he was wearing, streaked and dotted with dark-brown marks. He recognised them instantly. Dried blood.

"What does this remind you of?"

"An evidence bag," Howard said immediately. "You think DI Swift found something?"

"Looks that way. And he's done something to her to shut her up."

"Then why leave the evidence sitting on the table for us to find?"

Shawn's mind turned over the possibilities. "Or he used the evidence to get her here." The penny dropped. "Her finding evidence was never the problem. It was a trap from the start."

He did his best to rein in his emotions, when what he wanted to do was lash out, to kick at the wall and punch the table, and grab the nearest person and roar in their face. But he could do none of those things. "Fuck."

"Sarge, look." Howard nodded down to the kickboard. A slim mobile phone was flipped up against it, the screen cracked, as though it had been thrown or knocked out of someone's hand.

Shawn bent and picked it up. He didn't need to turn the phone on to see it was Erica's. There was a sticky mark on the back cover where Poppy had stuck several My Little Pony stickers onto Erica's phone in an attempt to make it 'pretty.' Shawn remembered how Erica had laughed about how she didn't think people would take a detective very seriously if she had a phone covered in pony stickers. It had rung when he'd tried her number back at the office. Had she been about to answer it, only Skehan had stopped her? Had he hit her?

That growingly familiar rage bubbled up inside him. If he was right in his suspicions that Skehan was responsible for the death of Naomi Conrad, then he was more than capable of killing Erica.

"Get an alert out, both on Brandon Skehan and DI Swift. Make sure everyone knows she might be in danger, or possibly hurt or worse." He swallowed down the wave of emotion that came with that thought. He couldn't imagine a world without Erica in it. He knew it wasn't comparable to her losing her husband—he and Erica were partners, but of a different kind to what she'd been with Chris—but the possibility of that hole in his life emerging felt like a cavernous sinkhole that he teetered on the edge of.

Where would he have taken her?

"He's copying her past cases and now he has her. What's he planning on doing with her?"

The letters to Nicholas Bailey. Why write to Bailey unless he was the key to all this?

Was Brandon Skehan planning on finishing what Bailey had started but had failed to achieve?

"I think I know where he might have taken her."

Erica had woken in the middle of a nightmare.

It was a nightmare she'd had multiple times since Chris's death, so many she'd lost count. Night after night, she'd jolted out of sleep, her heart crashing against her ribcage, her breath locked in her lungs, a scream trapped in the back of her throat.

But, other than that time with Chris, it had never been real before.

Now it was.

From somewhere nearby, a train rumbled and screeched through a tunnel. Hot air hit her face, and the floor was hard beneath her. When she blinked open her eyes, she stared into darkness.

Her mind went back to what had happened, piecing everything together. Brandon Skehan. He'd cut his own face and made himself look like a victim. He'd been the one to murder Naomi Conrad and then set fire to whoever the poor woman was who DI Carlton had been investigating. It wasn't only her past cases that he'd been copying, it had been one of the victims.

Where was he now?

She tested her arms and legs. She didn't think he'd tied her up. He must be feeling pretty confident that he'd got one over on her. She tried to sit up, but wooziness took over, and she had to force herself to keep still until it passed.

She remembered the tea she'd drunk. He must have put something in it. How stupid of her. She knew better than to put herself in such a vulnerable situation. But he'd seemed like a good bloke, and stupidly, she'd felt sorry for him. She'd really believed that he'd been traumatised by the attack.

Gradually, her eyes got used to the gloom.

"Good morning, princess," Brandon said from not far away. "Guess where we are?"

Was it morning already? No, she didn't think so. She hadn't been out of it for that long.

Erica pushed herself to sitting and coughed as acid rushed up from her stomach and burned the back of her throat. She didn't know what he'd given her in the tea, but it hadn't agreed with her.

"I know where I am," she managed to say.

"The same place your husband died." He sounded delighted with himself.

How was that possible? The abandoned Tube station had been bricked up after what had happened with Chris and Nicholas Bailey.

He read her thoughts. "It's taken me some time, I must admit. I've just been working on it, brick by brick, loosening each one and placing it back again so the Transport police wouldn't become suspicious."

She was back on that abandoned platform again. Tears of anger and frustration and grief rose to her eyes, but she blinked them away. There would be time for tears later.

"What are you going to do with me?"

A scraping met her ears, and a chink of light appeared, followed by another. He was unblocking the platform from the Tube line on the other side. They were right by the spot where Chris had died.

Erica wanted to scream.

She looked over her shoulder, trying to figure out how he'd got her in here in the first place. If he'd managed to drag her in, there must be a way out, too. That was what she needed to focus on. Getting out. But all that was behind her were more bricks. Some of them would be loose—enough that a person could fit through—she was sure of it, but it would take her time to figure out which ones, and she didn't think time was something she had on her side.

Had anyone realised she was missing yet? Yes, they must have. She'd been supposed to pick up Poppy, so Natasha would be worried by now. She'd probably call Shawn, wondering if they'd got caught up in a case. With a spark of hope, she remembered telling DC Rudd where she was going.

"You're not going to get away with this, you know," she said. "My colleagues know I came to see you."

He paused in unbricking the tunnel to glance over his shoulder at her. "But they won't know where you are now."

What had she done with her phone? She checked her pockets for it but then remembered dropping it back at the flat. Shit.

"Why are you doing this?" she dared to ask.

"You probably want some heart-wrenching story about how the police had terrorised me when I'd been younger, or that you reminded me of some parent who never loved me right. You want to understand me, Erica, don't you? But the truth is that you can't. I'm doing this simply because I can. The world bores me."

She remembered how Keith Allen from Forensic Submissions had said how psychopaths and sociopaths seemed like perfectly normal people on the surface and that people who considered themselves good judges of character had been taken in by them. They'd been talking about Robert Day at the time, though, not Brandon Skehan.

"So, this is all a game? A way of playing with us?"

"Not just you. Nicholas Bailey interested me. I thought it would be an...achievement...to finish what he started."

"By killing me?"

"Exactly."

"You're going to end up in prison."

"No, I won't. I have a second passport in a different name. I'll be gone the moment your heart stops beating."

"What?" Her sarcasm surprised her. "And not be around to get all the glory?"

"Good to see you still have your sense of humour, Erica, even after everything you've been through."

She gritted her teeth. "It's DI Swift to you."

He chuckled and continued working each brick out of the wall. Already, the gap was big enough to fit a small person through.

Each of the bricks was stacked on top of the other, she assumed to be replaced, later, covering his tracks. If she could get her hands on one of them, it would make a decent weapon.

A train suddenly rushed past, a blast of heat and energy filling the space, and Brandon let out a whoop of exhilaration. He turned to her, his one good eye wild with excitement.

"Can you feel that?" he exclaimed. "That rush of power? What a way to go."

Erica slowly got to her hands and knees. One of the bricks had slid from the pile and was closer to her than the others. All it would take was a well-aimed swing to the back of the head and she'd take him down.

Would she get there before he noticed her moving, though? Was it better to go slowly, or get fully to her feet and make a run to try to grab it?

Carefully, she got into a position like a sprinter about to start a race. She did her best to ignore the wave of dizziness that threatened to take over. Her heart pounded. She expected him to look back at her and see what she was doing, but he was distracted by his job. The gap was almost empty of bricks now.

She sucked in a breath, and with a sudden burst of speed, lunged for the nearest brick. Her fingers closed around the rough surface, and with a scream of fury, she swung it at the back of Brandon's head. The end of the brick connected with his skull, and he fell sideways.

He let out a grunt and put his hand to his head. He looked at the blood on his fingertips as though surprised she'd hurt him.

Shit, she hadn't managed to knock him unconscious. He was far bigger than her, and she was still groggy from whatever he'd put in her tea. If it came down to a one-on-one fight, she had a feeling she'd lose.

There was only one way to escape, and that was through the same hole he'd just cleared. The Tube line lay beyond. If she landed on the tracks, she'd be electrocuted. If she stayed, he'd kill her.

She decided to take her chance with the tracks.

Not giving herself any time to back out, she climbed over the side and dropped down. A startled mouse scurried away, her feet only narrowly missing it. In the distance, the thunder and rumble and screech of distant Tube trains filled the tunnels. Not this one, though. Not yet. They were on other lines.

"Bitch!" Brandon yelled from behind her.

She got moving, unsure where she was even going or what her plan was. The walls were lit, but only dimly. She was terrified she'd catch her foot on something and fall.

The thud of feet landing on concrete came behind her, and she turned to find Brandon giving chase.

Shit, shit, shit.

She was painfully aware that she was in a Tube tunnel. How much of the rails and wires beside her had electricity running through them?

Poppy, Poppy, Poppy, Poppy.

Her daughter was the thing front and centre of her mind. She couldn't let this lunatic make Poppy an orphan.

She glanced back again. Brandon was gaining on her.

How long until the next train came along? Three minutes? Less? She focused on putting one foot in front of the other.

A hand suddenly grabbed her hair, yanking her back. A scream burst from her lips, but she lashed out, swinging her arm backwards. Her elbow connected with the cut across his eye.

Brandon's head snapped back, his hands automatically going to his face. "Ah, fuck!"

Erica kept going, but things felt futile. Even though she'd hurt him, it had been a lucky strike. The moment a train came along this line, she was a goner. They both were.

She couldn't help checking on his position as he came after her. Blood soaked through the white bandages across his face.

The elbow she'd given him must have undone some of the stitches across the wound. It turned one half of his face red, even in the low lighting of the Tube tunnel, and it was terrifying.

Where was the train? Shouldn't one have come along by now?

The lights along the tunnel walls went dim.

Hands grabbed her from behind. "Got you now, bitch."

His knee struck the rear of hers, and her legs folded beneath her. His fingers were a clamp around the back of her neck, shoving her forward. The rail track was right beneath her. Erica fought against him, pushing with everything she had, but he was stronger. If he threw her on the line, she'd die.

His grip loosened, and she fell.

She hit the track, face first. Terror filled her. She was certain this would be her last moment, and hundreds of volts of electricity were about to course through her body.

"Police! Stay right where you are!" The shout echoed down the tunnel.

Relief flooded through her, and she found her voice. "Here! I'm over here. Brandon Skehan is here, too."

At the shout of 'police', Brandon had turned and run back in the direction they'd come. Feet thudded up the tunnel towards her.

"Erica?"

She recognised Shawn's voice, and a moment later, he was beside her, helping her up off the tracks.

"What happened?" she asked. "The tracks should have had electricity running through it."

"We held up the train at the previous station and switched the power off to this line."

"Oh God. I thought I was going to die. I thought I was never going to see Poppy again." She clutched at him. "How did you know?"

"He was copying your previous cases. I knew he'd bring you here. He wanted to finish off what Nicholas Bailey had started."

Shouts came from farther down the tunnel as uniformed officers caught up with Brandon. The light was good enough for her to make out them wrestling him to the floor and handcuffs being clipped around his wrists.

"It's okay," Shawn said, "they've got him. It's over."

Chapter Thirty-Three

E rica had wondered if he'd be willing to meet her. A week had passed since her abduction by Brandon, and she'd realised she wouldn't be able to rest until she closed this part of the case as well.

How much information had Nicholas Bailey been given about what had happened? He must have watched the news, but the details hadn't been shared to the national channels. Just an 'incident' in the same place a police officer's husband had been killed two years earlier.

She approached the legal visits room where she'd interviewed him before, but this time she wasn't nervous or anxious in any way. Instead, she walked with a straight spine and her chin lifted. Nicholas could have helped them catch Brandon, but instead, he'd chosen to put his own needs ahead of what was important.

Nicholas sat with his arms folded, his legs splayed out, the look of a sulky teenager across his face. He glanced over at Erica as she entered, and his lips tightened, his eyes narrowing.

He didn't speak.

"I wasn't sure you'd see me," she said, taking a seat opposite.

"Didn't realise I had much of a choice. You're the police, aren't you?"

"You had a choice. You could have refused me, but you didn't, did you, because you wanted to find out what happened."

"What happened about what? I don't know what you're talking about."

"You don't want to know what happened to the man who had been writing you those letters?"

His gaze flicked to hers, and then he sat up in his seat. He was interested. "Go on then, tell me."

"You didn't win, Nicholas. Brandon Skehan, the same man who called himself M Cimi or The Mimic, as he's now known, is in custody. You may even find yourself meeting him in person soon. As you can see, I'm very much alive, and Skehan won't be hurting anyone else ever again."

She'd looked up mimicry after DC Rudd explained to her what the name M Cimi had meant. She'd found a definition called aggressive mimicry, which was found in predators or parasites. It was where the creature shared the characteristics of a harmless species, allowing them to avoid detection. Initially, she'd thought he'd referred to himself as a mimic because he'd been copying her past cases, but in the end, she decided it was because he'd been mimicking one of his victims.

* * * *

LIFE FELL BACK INTO its usual routine—or at least as routine as it could be as a detective. She was up to her neck in paperwork when her DCI called her into his office.

"Everything okay, sir?"

"Take a seat, please, Erica." Gibbs gestured to the chair opposite his desk.

She sat and clasped her hands between her knees. "That sounds ominous."

"I just got news that Nicholas Bailey died in his cell last night."

Her mouth dropped open. "What? How?"

"Looks like suicide. He used an uncut length of zip he stole from the workshop."

Her mind reeled. "How is that even possible?"

"He tied the ends together and hung himself from the top rail of his bunk."

"I...I thought he was in a double cell? How did it happen without anyone noticing?"

"His cellmate didn't do anything to help. Says he was asleep when it happened, but apparently the two of them never really got along. There's no proof he had anything to do with it, or that he helped."

"Jesus Christ."

The strength went out of her body, the air leaving her lungs in a whoosh, and she found herself slumped in the chair. Her hand went to her mouth, and she stared down at the floor.

Gibbs frowned at her. "Are you okay?"

She nodded, not trusting herself to speak. She'd been there the other week. What had been her motivation for going? Just to rub it in?

"Was it me?" she said eventually. "Did I prompt him to kill himself?"

"Nicholas Bailey was a sick man. His cellmate says he was talking to someone in the end, as in, talking to someone who wasn't there. He said he kept calling the person Danny."

"Danny? You mean his brother?"

"That's right."

She remembered how he'd kept looking over at something she couldn't see. How he'd jumped at a noise she didn't hear. Had Nicholas been listening to the ghost of his brother the whole time? Not that Erica believed in such things—unless it was three in the morning and she was alone after just watching a scary film—but Nicholas had believed.

Had Danny been the one to encourage Nicholas to end things? Should there be some comfort that Nicholas had at least had the company of his brother in his final moments, even if it had all been in his head?

Whatever had happened, Nicholas Bailey was dead.

That part of her life was over.

Acknowledgements

I had a couple of new people helping me out on The Mimic, in particular with how day to day life went inside a prison. So, thank you to Ali Mountjoy and to David Monaghan-Jones for answering my numerous questions about all things related to prison life. I may have taken some liberties to make the storyline work, so anything that wasn't quite right is all down to me!

Thank you, as always, to my editor, Emmy Ellis, for working on yet another book for me. I don't know how I'd manage without you.

Thanks to Patrick O'Donnell, who runs the Cops and Writers facebook group, and who consults with me on the aspects of police procedural for this series. If you're a writer who needs help with their book, I highly recommend both the group and Patrick.

Thank you to my proofreaders, Tammy Payne, Jacqueline Beard, and Glynis Elliott for doing that final read through for me. Typos are like weeds, and I'm a terrible gardener!

And as always, lots of love and thanks to you, the reader, for reading my Erica Swift books. I hope you enjoyed The Mimic.

Until next time!

M K Farrar

About the Author

MK Farrar is the pen name for a USA Today Bestselling author of more than thirty novels. Though 'Some They Lie' was her first psychological thriller, it wasn't her last, and she's now written eight novels of crime and psychological fiction. When she's not writing, M.K. is rescuing animals from far off places, binge watching shows on Netflix, or reading. She lives in the English countryside with her husband, three daughters, and menagerie of pets.

You can sign up to MK's newsletter at her website, mkfarrar.com. She can be also be emailed at mkfarrar@hotmail.com. She loves to hear from readers!

Also by the Author

Crime after Crime series, written with M A Comley
Watching Over Me: Crime after Crime, Book One
Down to Sleep: Crime after Crime, Book Two
If I Should Die: Crime after Crime, Book Three
Standalone Psychological Thrillers
Some They Lie
On His Grave
In the Woods

www.ingramcontent.com/pod-product-compliance
Lightning Source LLC
Chambersburg PA
CBHW020908160726
47993CB00005B/1877